Team Savage

III

Ace Boogie

Team Savage III

Printed in the United States of America.

ISBN: 978-0-9992646-9-0

Made in the USA
Middletown, DE
19 April 2024

53231534R00137

Table of Contents

Chapter One

* * * * *

A t the end of a dark hallway a light beamed from the open door. A stained carpet riddled with piss, juice, and alcohol, lead up to the alumna living areas. Posters covered the walls to hind the holes punched into them by angry 15-year-old Marvell.

In the bedroom next door, a glass pipe was being inhaled on by his mother who'd been an addict for over twenty years. Marvell never knew the once clean, and beautiful queen his mother was back in the day. He never had the opportunity to witness her and any other position then as a drug addict, which made him never respect her. Marvell starred at the ceiling with hunger consuming his thoughts. He wondered how his mother always had money for drugs but never for food. Over the last few weeks, he'd been thinking about how he could change his misfortune. He had a few ideas, and they all had something to the with the occupation they consumed his neighborhood Allied Dr. This block was well known for criminal activities in Madison Wisconsin, and Marvell wanted in on it. He just didn't know where he'd get his start. Apart of him wanted to become a stick-up kid, but another wanted to be a drug kingpin. The music he listens to didn't help that even the slights bit. He played Lil baby and Lil Druk none stop, on his broke phone, dreaming of the day he'd be living a better life. Marvell stood up and looked out the second-floor window at a few hustlers pushing dope. He liked how fly their clothes were, unlike his own witch where hand me downs from an older cousin. Marvell couldn't even remember the last time he'd worn a new outfit and had enough of waiting on his no good as mommy to step in.

If his luck was gone change it was up to him to change it no one else. Marvell watched one of the drug dealers go to his car and place something under the driver seat before getting out. He watched him as he went back to join his friend.

Marvell wondered what it was he'd placed inside the car as the man walked down block.

This is my chance, he thought getting outta bed and going into the kitchen. He looked around for something to break the window and decided on a pip under the sink.

He grabbed it in ran back to his room to see where the drug pusher was. He spotted them a few houses down, and fathomed he had enough time to break into the car and make it back inside before they could catch him.

He took a few deep breaths and forced his self to open the front door and stepped out into the small hallway. He heard the sounds of sexual activities going on inside his neighbor's apartment as he rushed down the stair stratified, they were too busy fucking to become witness of the crime he was about to commit. Marvell stepped into the night, and cool air brushed the short dreadlocks from his dark handsome face. This tall frame aloud for his to rush the car and short strides. He stood Infront of the Jaguar F- Pace SVR and felt like a hater for what he was about to do.

But the hunger overpowered his conscious, and he slammed the poll into the window with all his might breaking the glass. Shield spilled on the pavement as Marvell went inside quickly going to where he saw the man hide something. He reached under the seat and felt cold steal. When he griped the dreko, he felt something else brush against his hand. The whole time his heart was beating outta his chest. He tucked the pistol on his waste before reaching back under the seat and grabbing a large amount of coke.

Marvel put it in his pocket and looked around, the coast was clear, so he got up and brushed the glass from his jeans and ran back to the house, his dreadlocks blowing in the wind. Once he was safely in his room, he sat on the bed outta breath.

Marvel looked out the window. The man was coming back up the block. He jumped off his bed and turned off his light not wanting to bring attention to his crib. He listened as the men talked amongst each other about the break end. One was laughing about the situation while the other was upset. The next thing he knew there were headlights before the sound of a car pealing out the parking lot. Marvell slowly went to the window and peaked out they were gone. He let out a deep breath once he noticed the scene was clear of everything but the glass from the busted window.

He sat back on the bed before hearing the sounds of a lighter being flicked. It was a sign his mommy was still getting high. The weight of the dreko in his waist band brought his attention to the contents he'd just acquired. Marvell pulled the drugs and gun out and lay them on the bed. He noticed the cocaine was packed in dime bags and counted them. It was a thousand dollars' worth. He couldn't help but smile, this was the first time he had anything close to a thousand dollars.

He looked at the gun in picked it up, in pointed it at the mirror and saw his reflection. He bit his bottom lip, and posed, and felt powerful for the first time in his life.

Then it hit him again, he didn't get any money. How would he get something to eat? One thing was sure McDonald's was gone accept crack for a big mic. There was a knock on his room door before he was able to hide the drugs his mommy entered his room.

Her eyes glowed at the sight of the drugs, "Where the fuck you get this," she asked. Coming over and attempting to grab his dope, Marvell slap her hand away.

"Fuck is wrong with you just walking in my room." He yelled at her while standing to his feet upset. His mommy step back afraid of him. "Marvell baby I wasn't gone take it I just wanted to look." She said in a submissive voice.

"This ain't none of yo muthefucin business so get the fuck out my room with yo hype ass," he yelled. She backed outta the room before saying, "let me get one of those for these 5 dollars."

Marvell didn't even hesitate to give the poison to the woman that birth him. The only thing on his mind was to feed the beasts within and the 5 dollars was good at McDonald's unlike the crack. He gave her the bag and took the dollar bills before rushing out the house. When he stepped outside, the crack in his pocket and pistol on his hips, he began to slowly make the walk to Micky D.

The streets were quiet allowing him to think while on his mission to eat. It felt good to have money in his pocket even if it was only a few dollars.

A blue van pulled up behind Marvell and he reached for the pistol. The white man inside put his head out the window, dumb to how close he'd come to getting it blow off.

"You working?" He asked looking around. Marvell looked around like he was talking to someone else. When he saw, he was the only person around, he asked, "what you say?"

"You working?" the man repeated. Marvell was lost, unable to understand. The man saw the confusion on his face and decided to ask the question flat out.

"You go rock?" He asked and that's when it hit Marvell, he was looking for crack. Marvell looked at him and wondered whether he was the police. He wasn't sure but decided if he was gone come up, he'd have to take a Chance.

"Ya, what up" he said. The white man glanced around again before telling Marvell to get in.

Marvell got in and they pulled off. The man drove while glancing over at him. He went and his pocket and pulled out the bundle.

"What you try'na do?" Marvel asked.

"I got $300 but I gotta test it and make sure its straight." The man said pulling out twenty dollars. He handed it to Marvell, "let me get one of them twenties."

Marvell gave him one of the dimes quickly recognizing the man was overpaying which he didn't have a problem with.

"Pull over to the McDonald's" Marvell said once he spotted it. The van quickly turned into the lot and Marvell looked on as he went in his pocket and retrieved a pipe and quickly open the bag and placed it on the glass dick and light it. He blew out the smoke and the car seemed to get 10 degrees hot. "This god shit let me get 14 more." He said going, in his pocket and pulling out the money and throwing in into Marvell's lap. He grabbed it and went in his jab and counted off 14 more slugs and handed them to the white man. Marvell reach for the door about to get out when he was stopped.

"You got a number?" the man asked.

"Fo what?" Marvell asked.

"So, I can call you in get some more," the man said noticing Marvell was new to hustling.

"Nuh but give me yours and I'll call you once I get one." Marvell said in an attempt to hold on to his first customer. The man wrote his name and number on a script piece of paper and handed it to Marvell.

Marvell stepped outta the car and watched as the man pulled off. He walked into McDonald's, the smell of food reminding him that he needed to take care of his stomach. He got in line behind a tall ugly ass woman, who couldn't make up her mind on what she wanted. She stood with her hands on her hips. Marvell went in his pocket and pulled out the 305 dollars, it was the most money he'd ever had. He stood tall, with his spirits high. Feeling wealthy, the money gave him a high like no other. Marvell stepped up to the counter and placed his order for a Big Mac, before going to take a seat.

He unwrapped the Burger with quickness and precision as Mike Tyson throws a left hook. And three and a half bites later it was gone. Marvell reclined back and slowly picked at the rest of the meal, while contemplating his next move. One thing was certain he needed to get a phone ASAP. Another was finding new customers, something his mother hype ass could help with. He took a sip from the soda, before getting up and throwing it away, and leaving the store. Once the cool air brushed against his face, he inhaled it before starting the walk to the BP gas station to buy a prepaid mobile phone. The stroll didn't take long, and when he walked on the parking lot it was packed with nice cars and sexy women. Dude sat on top of their wipes smoking blunts. He watched as a beautiful light skinned girls got up on top of a car to dance. Her ass was so fat, that the thugs begin to pull money from their pockets and throw it at her. Marvell watched the show a while before the police pulled up and order people to move around, which he did remembering the illegal drugs in weapon in his procession.

When he entered the store, the Arabic owner greeted him by name. "How are you doing today Marvell?" He asked in a heavy accent.

"I'm aight, try'na get one of them prepaid phone that's it." He said going in his pocket and pulling out his cash. The Arabic grabbed the phone and place it on the counter. "will this be all?" He asked.

"Nah, I need one of them $50 minute cards." Marvell watched as he retrieved the car and paid the total, before leaving. When he stepped outside, he noticed a blue Jeep and strolled up to it, excited to see his big homie TT. Even though TT was only 3 years older than him, Marvell always looked up to him. He'd been getting money since he was Marvell's age.

"What good snake?" TT asked Marvell.

"Shit T," Marvell responded putting his hand through the window to shake up.

"Where you heading?" TT asked, while blowing out a cloud of some.

"To the house. Why you gone give me a ride?" Marvell questioned trying to avoid the long walk home.

"Ya I got you Tee, get in."

It didn't take but a second for Marvell to jump inside. TT tried to pass him the blunt, but he declined against drugs use. He'd made a promise to his self to never use drugs, after the effects they had on his mother. TT understood, and pulled off, he turned up the music, and sat back in his seat like the coolest nigga in the world and Marvell peeped his swag and wanted to be just like him. They pulled up to his apartment building and TT stopped the car short of the glass, Marvell had broken." what the fuck is this?" He asked.

"Ion know, you know how the Drive be," Marvell lied, while referring to Allied Dr, which had a repetition for being the ghetto.

"On MC you ain't lying." TT said letting out a light giggle as Marvell got out the car.

"Aright Tee," TT added before pulling out the lot.

Marvell rushed back to his home and into his room to program his new phone and begin his claim from this hell hole.

* * * * *

The sunshine through the otherwise dark bedroom of a majestic estate on 7 lush acres. The fine home had an entry hall with mahogany staircase along with magnificent fireplaces sunrooms, swimming pool and so much more. But it did little to brighten the mood of the man who lay in bed with a wondering mind, and a heavy heart. The secret he'd been keeping was leading him to view his wife in an unpleasant manure.

Three months passed since Danjunema's daughter Bee was shot down in the streets of Madison, Wisconsin. He thanked god she was still alive, even if she was in a coma.

Kia still didn't know he discovered her secret. Back when she was a teen, he forced Kia to have sex with him, as payment for a debt, she found out she was pregnant two months later. Once she told her mother, she was given to options. The first was to get an abortion, the second was to live on the street. Kia chose the latter and moved out.

She planned to keep the baby, but found life on her own hard to withstand, and did the unthinkable.

Danjunema learned the secret, while lying in bed with her while she had a nightmare.

When she woke up, tears rain down her face, and said she was sorry.

He asked why?

But she didn't respond, just gave him a blink stare. Danjunema choose not to push her and left it alone for the moment.

But couldn't disregard her screaming, "how could I get pregnant, my first time." Danjunema was a believer that dreams cast into reality.

The next day, he had his people inspect the situation and found out about his daughter. The discovery was mind blowing. He couldn't think of a way to bring it up to Kia, or a way to walk into the life of his child. He had his team follow Bee, and that's when he discovered she murdered two kids.

After that he kept an eye on her, as he thought of a way to introduce himself to his only child. He looked over at his wife, she was sound asleep in their home.

After Bee was shot, his team took her to a hospital in Chicago. They stopped to wash her hands with bleach to remove any gunpowder.

Danjunema went to visit her every day, but she was still unresponsive. The longer he went without telling Kia he knew about their daughter while she was in the hospital fighting for her life, the more it was killing him inside. He wondered how Kia could lay in his bed with such a secret, without feel guilty. It was this thought that made him second guessing their newfound love. If she was capable of something like this what else was possible. How could a mother abandon their only child? He just didn't understand it!

This type of shit only happened in movies. Not real life. He was a control freak, and not being able to help his baby girl while she was fighting for her life was killing him. He might've been powerless over her fight to live, but he had one good thing going for him. He'd just learned who might've been responsible, after months of searching. His team discovered she'd shot Cash, a major drug lord in Chicago.

He also unearthed that Cash was friends with the person who'd shot his child. Putting them together was enough information to start a war.

A hundred of Africa best slayers were brought into America through the Mexico border. He'd been waiting and this morning received the call this army had arrived. *It was time to play war games,* he thought getting outta bed in placing a soft kiss on Kia's cheek.

She rolled over and smiled at him.

"Hi daddy," she said.

"How are you feeling beautiful? " he asked.

"Wonderful, as long as you're the first thing I see in the morning," she said from her heart.

Kia loved him, no matter if she cheated a million times, he had her heart now and forever.

Danjunema went into the restroom as Kia watched. She sat up in bed pulling the covers up over her naked breast. Her thought went to the dream she had last night.

It haunted her most of her adult life, but lately she'd had it most nights. Kia regretted the decision to abandon her child the split second after she'd done it. But never went back. A part of her felt the girl was better off without a drug lord as a father, and a mother that didn't want her.

At that time, the baby only reminded her of being forced to have sex. When the decision was made, she would've never imagined all these years later she'd be married to Danjunema.

God was giving her a signal something was wrong with her child. Kia needed to locate her but didn't know where to begin.

* * * * *

Marvell eyes popped open at the loud scream of a woman voice outside. He sat up and glanced around the filthy room while whipping the cold out the side of his eyes. The woman's voice could be heard as she pleaded to someone to stop hitting her. He stood and strolled over to the window and peeked out.

What he saw, caused him to rush to retrieve the dreko from under his bed. He put his shoes on as quick as possible and rushed downstairs. When he exited the building, his mommy was on the ground as a man stood over her about to deliver a kick to her face. But before he was able to, he heard the building door slam shout. Marvell noticed the same man he'd robbed last night was beating his mother.

"Hit her again pussy!" Marvell said waving the gun at him. The man raised his arms in the air surrendering. His mother was on the ground with her eyes closed and her hands covering her head. The sight pissed him off even more." Get yo ass up!" He yelled at her while holding the man at gunpoint.

At the sound of her son's voice, she opened her eyes. Once she saw it was safe, she rose to her feet. Marvell spotted the fat lip and bloody noise and became furious.

"Go yo ass in the house," he said, and like a child she ran inside. Marvell walked over to the guy and slapped him in the face with the firearm knocking him to the pavement.

"Shit," he yelled at the pain that shot through his head, while grabbing his noise.

"You like hitting women huh?" Marvell yelled striking him once more. "Lay face down pussy." He added. The dude mean mugged him before slowly putting his face in the pavement and his arms out. Marvell stood over his back and patted him down and found a gun in his left pocket and tucked it on his waist band. Marvell went back in his pocket and found a stack of bills and some coke. He took them both before telling him to stand up and get the fuck off his block. The man slowly did as he was instructed. He looked at Marvell studying his face for a later date. Marvell peeped this and decided to make an example outta him. He told him to turn and walk away which he did. But before he exited the parking lot Marvell shot him once in the ass and watched as he ran off holding the wound.

"On MC, next time I catch you over here I'm gone kill yo bitch ass!" He yelled, while laughing. He looked up at his apartment and noticed his mom looking out the window. He shook his head at her, believing whatever provoked the attack was her fault. He tucked the gun, before taking off running to his sister house.

Meanwhile

A twin-size mattress occupied the corner along with a few chairs in the basement. The concrete floor was clean like the rest of the house, and a flat screen TV was mounted to the wall, but other than these items the house was empty. Black sat in the basement in Riverdale IL, as June walked down the stairs. The last few month she spent with him wasn't that bad, he fed her and never once tried to rape or harm, her in anyway. The only problem was she wasn't allowed to leave. He'd moved her all over Illinois in this time, and she never once tried to escape. A part of her enjoyed being with him. He was one of a kind, in made her laugh, like never before. Based off how they acted, no one would guess he'd kidnapped her.

When June marched into the room Black was beaming glad to have some company. "Where my food a nigga?" she wisecracked like they were old friends. June pulled it from behind his back in handed it to her. "You know I ain't gone leave you in this bitch hungry," he said taking a seat on the bed next to her. Black glanced up at him, they starred into each other eyes. There was some fondness there between them. But neither acted on it. June couldn't bring himself to make a move on a woman he'd kidnapped and held against her will. He wasn't that type of nigga.

He regretted taking her in the first place, but his emotions got the best of him. The losing Kim, had him out of his mind. He wasn't himself when he made the decision to take her.

"A Black, I been thinking, and you can leave! I just need you to remember you got a body under you belt as well. You butchered one of Cash girls, and if he finds this out, he ain't gone forgive... So, it's best you stay far away from him, and never tell anyone, what took place at that crib." He said.

Black just starred, speechless. *Shouldn't she be happy, why was she feeling abandoned?* It was because they'd grown close over the last few months, and she cherished being around him.

Where would she go? She perceived June was right, Cash would want answers, like how she survived. Where had she been the last few months and so much more. A while back, June told her Bee was in the wind in he couldn't locate her anywhere.

Black was glad to hear this information, as long as he couldn't find Bee, she was alive.

"What if I don't wanna leave?" She asked. June glared at her baffled, why would she want to say?

"Don't worry Black on Dave I won't kill you... It's okay to go home. You ain't gotta worry about nothing happen to you." He said hoping to ease her anxiety.

"I want to stay!" She repeated," I have nowhere to go, and I know this sounds crazy, but I feel safe with you." She said, as they held eye contact. Black cast away, before digging into the bag to see what he bought her. Once she noticed it was sharks inside her stomachache, shit, she ain't even know she was this hungry.

June looked at her a moment longer before saying, "You can stay if that's what you want, but not here in Chicago... If you want, you can go with me to Beloit, Wisconsin," he said putting his hands in his pocket. He was uncomfortable with her decision to stay. He was ashamed of taking her and was looking forward to ridding his conscious of that lack of judgement. Black beamed; grateful he was gone to keep her around. This was a new beginning, no matter how it came about, she was thankful for it. Black told herself she wanted to be loyal to whatever it was they had going on. She'd disappointed Bee,

Glory and even Cash. She was looking forward to proving to herself she wasn't a Jinx's. Starting today she desired to turn things around.

"Ok when do we leave?" She asked smiling. June stared, unable to apprehend why she didn't want to leave. What he didn't comprehend was she didn't have a life to return to. She was a loner now, no friends and know family. It was weird but he was all she had, and she craved to hold on to what little she did have.

"Shit we can leave now!" He said, Get yo shit in meet me outside." He added, turning and walking out the room.

Black watched as he exited. She peeked around the basement before slowly standing to her feet and grabbing what little belongings, she had and followed him out.

Meanwhile
Chicago – Cash

The dark blue interior leather seats were customized and made for a king. It matched the black and blue paint on the Land Rover Range Rover Sport SVR. It was one of many automobiles owned by the king of Chicago, Cash. The supercharged engine made him feel safe enough to escape from any situation. He was out the hospital and back in the streets like nothing ever happened. That shooting at the club only made him feel unbreakable. Over the last three months he was able to get over the loss of his girls and childhood friend Reese. But that was the game for you, it didn't take long for people to forget and move on with life. The only massacre he wasn't over was his brother. But as time passed, he learned there was no leads to be discovered and whoever killed him was a professional.

It was time for life to move on, his promises to his mother weren't forgotten, but on hold. When the time came, and he discovered who was responsible, the hit would happen, and a promise would be fore filled. But at the moment it was time to enjoy being alive. *Who else but the one In only true king could servile behind hit like that,* he thought. Cash made a left turn on 85 in Morgan to link with Yangba. He was there expecting to do busines with him. Cash was alone, but he wasn't lacking, not even a little bit. He was holding his 40. With a drum ready for anything that came his was. The bitch at the club, would be the last to hit with that hot shit. *Next time he got done bad he was taking somebody with him,* he thought. As he pulled over once he saw Yangba in front of a house. Yangba was dark skin about 6'3 and 200 pounds. He was well known throughout Chicago for being a shot caller, and just as important for being quick to drill something himself. There was a gang of people around him and Cash ashamed they were Moe's. Yangba made his way to the vehicle in got in. The sound of "that" poured from the speakers. *Why you playing with my shorty like he won't come up out that cut? Why you talking' out your neck like he won't turn your ass to run? They say why we ain't kill his ass? We was on his ass for a couple months.*

"What good bro," Yangba said getting in the car and closing the door. He noticed Cash hold a pistol on his lap but wasn't worried. He learned about Cash getting shot up in Milwaukee, shit the whole city new this transpired. He chunked it up as Cash being on point.

"Shit...." Cash said looking over his shoulders.

"You good! " Yangba said hoping to ease his nerves.

"I'm good everywhere!" Cash said grabbing his pistol even harder. Yangba smiled, at the slick as comment, but let it go, he was try'na get plugged in, and wasn't gone let his pride get in the way of getting money.

"Nah, I wasn't saying it like that! But I feel you.... What's good though you said you had a business proposition?" Yangba said anticipating moving things alone, before they had to leave Cash slumped in his car with his brains blown out.

"Ya, I'm try'na get my coke out this way in I heard you the man to talk to..." Cash said relaxing just a little bit.

"What you talk bout, let me know what deal you got on the table?"

"We start off like this, whatever you by I front you! Then if that goes good, just hit you with em." He said peeking over his shoulders again. Yangba laughed inside. *Them shell a get a nigga mind right,* he thought.

"They gone be like the ones I'm hearing about?" He asked.

"Ya the same shit.... I don't play know games; my name speaks for itself!" Cash said.

"Ya you got that! People talk about how you do good business...." Yangba said, while doing some math in his head before adding, "Cool then, I'm gone take 5," he said.

"Say know mo I'm gone have folks, get up with you later on... " Cash responded.

"Say know mo," Yangba said, opening the door and stepping out the car. As soon as his feet hit the floor Cash sped off like a bat out of hell. He wasn't chancing someone making a move once Yangba was no longer in the automobile. Once he made it a few blocks away he slowed down the supercharged engine and glanced at his Patel watch. People could say he was acting like a hoe or whatever, but he was acting like a man with something to lose. Some would caution if he really felt this way, he'd have protection with him, but last time he was with 40 nigga's and still got shot up. So, it didn't matter to him anymore, he was gone put in his own work. Fuck he looked like paying nigga to protect him that were incompetent.

He planned on watching his own back in when that time came, he die in the streets before someone got off on him.

When he glared out his rearview mirror, he saw a black van accelerated behind him. He clinched his pistol tighter when he noticed the passenger window roll down.

Damn, he thought. His hand began to shack, and he began to sweat all over. When the vehicle got closer, he put the .40 up the window just in case he had to blow it. But the van went right pass him without the passenger looking his way.

The dark skin of the driver got his attention. *Damn dude black as a bitch,* he thought.

The instant the notion left his mind his passenger side window exploded.

Bloc! Bloc! Bloc! Bloc!

Cash felt a bullet knock the hat of his head just as he docked. But that didn't stop him from returning fire.

Boom! Boom! Boom! Boom! Boom! He peeked up and shot back. Cash wasn't about to lose his life like this. Not without holding his own. He pushed on the brakes as the pursuing car flew pass. He jumped out as the drivers of both vans stop. All doors opened, but the driver's doors and out jumped 6 masked man.

Boom! Boom! boom! Boom!

Cash discharged a few shots and began to run down the block, as the masked man gave chase. His heart was beating a hundred miles an hour as bullets flew past him hitting everything he passed. A woman screaming was all he heard, as he made it to the end of the blocks and saw Yangba in the Moe's running his way. *Damn* he thought it was a hit. But before he could raise his pistol, they began to engage the masked man for him. At that moment, the block turned into a warzone.

Yangba grabbed him by the jacket in pulled him towards an alley to an awaiting car. Once they were inside the car speed away.

"Who the fuck was that?" Yangba asked, as he heard the gunfire continue, as they escaped. It sounded like bombs were going off. It was at this point Yangba realized he'd abandon his man.

"I don't know who the fuck that was! Shit I ain't gone lie I thought it was you." Cash said holding his firearms tight in his hand.

Yangba screwed his face up at the comment but let it go.

"Nah that wasn't me. But whoever it was came to get rid of you." He said as they made a sharp left turn that cause them both to lean over, in their seat.

"Where you going?" Yangba asked, his mind on his guy back at the gunfight. The assassin in him was clashing with the captain inside. He knew rescuing Cash would get him that pug, he'd always wanted but at what cost?

"Take me to 95th and Dean Ryan I'm gone have somebody pike me up there," cash responded, placing his pistol on his lap in pulling out his phone." A skud send a few of the guys to pick me up on 95th, we at war." He said before hanging up.

Shit I guess it's time for bullets and gun smoke. He thought.

* * * * *

At a small duplex apartment on the westside of Madison. The house was quiet as an elderly woman lay sound asleep in bed, peacefully dreaming of her son, Money. She walked and held hands with him, happy god allowed her to dream he was alive.

"Ma, the time is coming for us to always be together." He said glaring into her eyes." Don't worry it's not as bad as it may seem, just make sure you repent, before you take yo last breath. It gone allow the lord to wrap his arms around you. I'm sorry I can't be there to protect you, but once you're here I'll be able to keep an eye on you." He added as tears rolled down his face.

"What are you talking about Milton?" She asked, calling him by his birth name. She was confused, as they starred into each other eyes. Her motherly instinct kicked in, and she wiped the tears from his face. "He coming momma!" He added giving her a tight hug. "Don't worry it don't hurt, just remember to repent momma. Make sure you repent," he said pulling away to stare at her one last time.

"Who's coming baby?"

"Lucifer," he whispered looking around. She saw the look of terror on his face.

"It's okay baby yo with god now. He welcome you in his home..... You don't have to worry about them streets know more. God loves you!" She said placing a hand on his face.

"He not coming for me mama, he coming for you!" He whispered.

At that instant she felt short of breath and began to wake up. When she opened her eyes, a hand was placed over her nose and mouth stopping her from breathing. At pair of yellowish eyes glared down on her.

Fright plugged her but she didn't fight. No, she closed her eyes in began to prey expecting to save her soul. Her son's words ring through her ears. Repent momma don't forget to repent!

The cold feeling on steel was place on her forehead, and she let out a scrap breathe. "God have Mercy on my soul," she said.

Bloc! Bloc!

The gunman projected two shots into her face blowing her brain all over the pillow.

Meanwhile
Kia

The Real Housewife's of Atlanta played on the TV, and the sounds of auguring came outta it, as the women fought like always. For the TV to be as loud as it was, the noise fell on deft ears as Kia paid it no attention. She spent the day in bed, she wasn't in the mood currently to do anything. Her heart was injured, something inside, said her baby needed her.

But where to begin? She had no idea! She began to wonder how her child look today. She was such a beautiful baby, with Chubb checks and wild eyes. Kia would never forget them eyes. A lonely tear escaped as she thought about something, she'd forced herself to forget all these years. No one new about this child! She wonders if she should confess to her husband. But didn't know how he'd react. He was a coldblooded executioner and a betrayal like this could cost her, her life. No, she wouldn't, at less not now. When the time was right, she'd get help locating their daughter.

But now she needs to get motivated to get money. The last few mouths she'd plunged into a routine of letting her friends run the operation. She still hadn't called June, even though she intended on it. Kia picked up her phone and dialed the prepaid burner phone she gave him a few months ago. Hopefully, he kept it after all this time. She put the phone up to her ear and waited as it rang.

"Hello" June answered.

"Meet me in Madison tomorrow, to discuss work together." Kia said getting straight to the point.

"Just send the location!" June said try'na hold back the excitement in his voice.

Without responding Kia hung up the phone and threw it on the bed. She began to wonder about the light skinned man. June was fine but not her type, she loved them dark, and tall. But at this point she just wanted some good dick something her husband could never provide. She laughed inside when she realized the real reason, she'd finally called him. It had nothing to do with business.

She wanted to see if the dick was as big as the print, she spotted last time they saw one other.

Damn, I'm a hoe, she thought. But good dick was hard to come by, and she hoped she'd located some. Maybe he could put her to sleep and halt the nightmares she's been having. Who knew, but she'd soon find out.

* * * * *

June and Black checked into a hotel when they made it to Beloit a few hours ago. June threw the phone on the bed and jumped up smiling from ear to ear.

Black lay back in bed on Facebook with the phone June bought her today. She glared at him like he was insane.

"What got you so glad?" She asked.

"Man skud, I can't tell you but know I been waiting on this a long time. I just got some news that can turn my whole world around.

"Why you keep calling me skud? Like I'm a dude. I'm a woman June!!!" She expressed. June paused and looked her up and down wondering where this was coming from. She was frowning at him with a serious expression, so he knew she wasn't joking.

"I don't know I guess it's something the guys be saying. It's out of habit, not disrespect," he said.

Black looked up at him before saying, "well I ain't yo skud! It ain't plight to call a woman something you call the guys.... On the ride up here, you said speak my mind, well that's what I'm doing," she said smirking. June shook his head respecting her wishes.

On their way to Beloit, he confessed that he felt uncomfortable being around her after the kidnapping. June said if she wanted to be around him, she'd have to behave like a free person. It made him smile, she was a quick learner. *Maybe she would be useful,* he thought.

His phone ring, he peeked at the screen in saw it was his big hommie calling.

"What good Cash?" He answered.

"Where you at folk's.. Somebody tried getting me out the way." Cash yelled in the phone, emotionally.

"I'm outta town skud, what happened???" June replied.

Not on this phone skud! Get back to the city now!" Cash yelled in the phone with aggression. June wasn't feeling his tone and he had business to take care of before returning to Chicago.

"Bro I got a few things to take care of then-"

"Nah nigga fuck that, get down here now or you can get done like killa..." Cash yelled cutting him off, and regretting the statement instantly.

"What you saying pussy? You had something to do with little bro murder?" June shouted grabbing the handle of his pistol. Black jump at the change and tone. The last time he was angry a whole house was wipeout.

"What you just say little nigga?"

"You heard me pussy! You had something to do with my little bro murder?" June repeated.

"Nah I didn't...... but if you wanna live don't return to my city!" Cash threatened.

"Fuck yo pussy I go where I want when I want nigga. On Dave when I see you, I'm putting you down." June yelled, mad as hell, Cash was coming at him like he was a hoe.

"Cool lil nigga it's a greenlight on you. You'll be with killa before for you know it. Don't worry I got yo momma. She gone be strength." Cash said.

"What pussy?" June asked, but the phone went dead. He frowned at it, try'na make since of what just materialized. Black starred at him as he looked discombobulated.

"You ok? " she asked. June took a seat, on the bed across from her. "Damn" he yelled. A tear rundown his face and he quickly wiped it away. Cash made him so mad he wanted to rush back to Chicago and murk him tonight. June wasn't stupid and knew what he'd got himself into. It was a war that would almost be impossible to prevail. He ignored Black's question as so many things hobbled through his mind. He tried to slow it down by taking a few deep breathe. But it wasn't working he had to act fast. He picked up his phone and called his mother.

"Hi baby," she said with excitement in her voice.

"Ma it's a code red! I need you to get outta the city. Remember how this work right?" He asked.

"Ya I do baby! Are you OK?" His mother asked bothered.

"Ya ma I'm good. Just do that in call me as soon as you make it out the city limits. Don't take nothing, just go this ain't a game."

I know baby, I know, we been over this. I love you and be safe." She said, more worried about his safety then her own."

"Love you to ma!" He said hanging up the line.

Black sat quiet letting him think. She was concerned with what just happened but if he wanted her to know he'd tell her. So, for right now she'd give him space. She perceived he was buddies with Cash, but there was nothing friendly about that conversation.

June stood there preparing himself for what was to come. It was time to boss up if he wanted to win this war. He would need to get his money all the way up to beef with somebody like Cash. The call from Kia came just in time. He couldn't wait until there meeting; he would do anything to get this plug. He glanced up at Black; she looked concerned. *Damn, what the fuck I'm gone do with this girl?* He thought, nervous for her wellbeing. Cash would put anyone down who was caught with him, no one would be spared. He went in his pocket pulling out 10 thousand and handed it to her. "I'm gone take care of some business. It's gone take me awhile. This should hold you over until I come back." He said looking into her eyes.

Black rolled her eyes at him, feeling abandoned again.

"What that for?" June asked.

"I ain't slow," she said, putting the money under the pillow.

"I never said you was! What the fuck you on?"

"Look boy, I know you giving me this money cause you ain't coming back." She said laying back in bed.

"That ain't the case. I plan on coming back, but life ain't promised. I could be gone at any moment. So, if I don't come back, you'll be able to get something going for yourself." He said sitting on the bed next to her. Black grasp everything he said. He seemed sincere. The thought of him not coming back affrighted her.

"I could come watch yo back." She said sitting up crossing her legs Indian style. June smiled her statement made him think of Kim.

"I can't let you do that. But it's nice to know you'd ride for a nigga." He said placing his hand on her knee. Black bent forward and kissed him. June pulled away and looked at her stunned. He looked at the beautiful girl before him. His dick was hard, but he wasn't sure this was right. He stood up, as Black starred at him with lust in her eyes. She wanted him for sometime now, and the idea of him perishing give her the courage to make a move.

She stood up and walked over to him as he stood there. Tip toeing close and pressed her body close to his. She felt his dick press against her; it felt huge. Black stood on her tiptoes and kissed him again. This time he returned her affection. June picked her, up in placed her on the bed. They continued to kiss passionately. He broke the kiss, unable to continue. He grabbed his keys and hurried out the room. Black lay back on the bed sexually frustrated, and dissatisfied.

* * * * *

Cash was disappointed he let his emotions cause him to threaten June. He wanted to call back and apologize but couldn't bring himself do so. A few minutes ago, he put the greenlight out on June, because he wasn't to be taken lightly his murder game was serious. This war with June was likely to turn some of his team against him. June was beloved amongst their gang.

This consideration alone was the reason Cash set up a meeting with Yangba. He didn't know if he could trust his nigga's until June was gone. The game was cold, and someone might set him up, and get him outta the way. *Nah a nigga won't be setting me up*. He thought. He was gone surround his self with a new group of people, that befit more from having him alive then dead. His thought switched to who just tried having him disseminated. He remembered the dark skin of one of the drivers, he appeared to be African. He wasn't beefing with any Africans. *Shit he ain't even know no Africans.* He thought. Then it hit him, but now they never had problems, even though they were both big in Chicago, they sold two different products. They sold heroin, and he pushed coke, which allowed them both to grow without bumping heads Nah Danjunema ain't have a reason to get him killed. But he was gone search into it, just in case.

If he was responsible the street of Chicago was able to become a warzone.

Cash was beefing on too many fronts. It seems like god was ready to collect his soul, cause a lot of shit was coming his way. He was try'na turn a new leaf when he was shot down. Now all this was transpiring. Maybe it was time to leave the game behind. The street wasn't showing the same love as it used to.

He needed out but his dignity wouldn't let anyone force him out. If he left it would be on his own free will. He lost to much and gave too much to let someone hoe him now.

Chapter Two

* * * * *

As the sun roles a tall young man walked past his neighbor's house and noticed her door was slightly open. He stopped and turned towards the home, something inside pulled him towards the door.

"Your door is open miss Moore!" He yelled out. When no one responded he push the door open, "Ms. Moore are you ok?" He asked before marching in the house. A strange feeling came over him, something felt amiss. The house was frigid and dark. He made his way through the living room, and thought about turning back, but *what if Ms. Moore needed his help. He thought. What if she'd fallen and couldn't get up?* "Is anyone home?" He yelled. Still no response. He looked up the long hallway, and the door at the end was open. He took an endless breath when he saw Ms. Moore lying in bed. "Ms. Moore, your door is open." He repeated for what felt like the hundred time. When she didn't budge, he knew something was vile. *Damn Miss Moore must have passed away in her sleep* he thought as he walked in the room. What he faced made him throw up the pancakes he ate that morning.

* * * * *

The inside of the suite was nice enough but was nothing compared to the ones in Chicago. There was a hot tube, and all, but it could've been better. Just the whole set up, of the hotel didn't feel right. *Whoever the interior designer was needed to step their game up,* June thought. Last night he drove to Madison and got a room. He ruminated about Black, Kia, and the war with Cash. His mother called him, informing him, she made it out the city which was a relief. He called Kutta in Bullet, the only people he trusted. The one thing that was bananas about beefing with yo guys was you didn't know who was on who side. Kutta in Bullet had loyalty to him, but cash had enough money to turn yo momma against you.

June rolled over in bed when the burner phone on the nightstand ring.

"Hello?" He said, sound asleep.

"Did you make it to Madison yet?" Kia questioned.

"Ya I made it last night." He said getting out of bed, while whipping the cold from the side of his eyes.

"Where you staying." She asked, "I'll meet you there," she added.

"I'm at the Best Western on gammon rd. He said.

"OK I ain't to far from there, I'mma be pulling up in 5 minutes. What room you in?" She seeked.

June didn't like to tell her his location, but he wasn't in the position to be picky.

"214!" He said grabbing his pistol and taking it with him to the bathroom. He was on high alert until the meeting was over with. When she was gone, he would rest. June got himself together, before there was a light knock on the door. He went to it, gun in hand squinted out the peephole. Kia posted there alone looking like a snack. He opened the door and Kia tramped in like she owned the place. Her fragrance flooded the space, and he stole a peek at her fleshy ass. *Damn this bitch bad.* He thought as Kia took a set on the bed.

"I'm gone get to the point. I need some good dick! If you can provide it, I'll provide all the coke you can handle." She said as she began to undress. June stood at the door holding it before allowing it to close.

If all he had to do was fuck her proper to get plugged, consider it done. He walked over to Kia as she took off her dress. He starred at her body as she stood before him.

His cock began to thicken at the sight of her. Kia placed her arms around him. *He was fine as hell* she thought. June picked her up and laid her back on the bed.

He stood up and began to undress. When he pulled his briefs off, Kia mouth fell open at the sight of his 12inch cock. June smiled, it never got old seeing the reaction when a woman first saw it. He dropped to his knees eyeing her pussy. June wasn't really into eating pussy, but today he was gone to put is all into it and try to suck the soul outta her. He consumed her pussy, nipping at her clitoris. He greedily sucked on her, and notice, how long it's been since he'd last done so until now. He hadn't had sex since Kim was murdered. Just the taste of Kia was enough to drive him insane.

"Yes, oh yes. Suck my clit," she yelled just, as he placed it in his mouth. Kia's pussy was hungry and wet, and she was ready for more than having it ate.

"Okay, it time to see what up with that dick!" She said pulled his face from her pussy by his dreads. June stood up, and Kia watched as he rubbed the head of his dick over her cat a few times. He carefully pushed is it inside her pussy. Her breathe was taking away as she watched inch after inch disappear. When he was about 8 inches' inside, she felt overstuffed like never before. Kia wrapped her arms around his back as he began fucking her. Within seconds they were going at it like crazy. June held back as he fucked her tight hole. *She got that wet wet,* he thought as he low stroked her. Kia continued to scream out to fuck her harder. She was driving him crazy.

"Pull out, pull outttt." She said.

June snatched out confused in dissatisfied. But Kia had him turn on his back. She wanted to taste herself on his beautiful cock. June watched as she placed his dick in her mouth. She attacked it like a lioness and sucked it like crazy. She made a show of gobbling his tasty stalk of flesh. Kia head game was out his world. She had his toes curling. He put his hands on the back of her noggin and began to glid her up in down. She treasured the fill of the long poll against her tongue. When she looked up his eyes was sealed, he was in heaven.

June glace down at Kia; she was a beast. She smiled with his cock in her mouth before trying to deep throat it.

"Damn shorty. You go some good ass top! " he said enjoying her mouth.

Kia pulled away, she placed a kiss on the head of his dick before straddling him and putting his cock in her. She was so wet he slid in in one stroke.

"Damn you so deep! " she said, as she began to ride him, on her tiptoes and bounce up and down. June held her hips forcing her to come all the way down. Every time he hit the bottom of her pussy, she leaped up like a bout of lighten had struck her. The pain felt so good, that she began to have back-to-back orgasm. When she felt June, poll began to scell she jumped up in placed him in her mouth. He exploded and Kia sucked until he was begging her to stop. Then she pulled his cock from her mouth and placed it on his thigh. June settled there with his eyes close as Kia got up and put her dress back on. She wiped her mouth before saying, "I'll have someone drop a brick off here, and we'll go from there depending on how you act." She said walking towards the door. "I'm gone need that dick on call, in exchange for doing business with you, "she added. June sat up, "I need more than one! I need ten, and I'm paying up front," he said. Kia turned around, "that's cool, pay up front! But I still want you on call." She said licking her lips. June smirked; he didn't have an issue with that. "Cool, just hit me," he said as she walked out the room.

* * * * *

Marvell left his sister house after counting the 5,000 dollars and weighing the '63' he took of the man yesterday. He spent the night over her house. After his sister heard what he'd done she took their mom someplace safe.

She let him have it, for leaving her at the same place he committed a robbery. Marvell's young mind allowed for the mistake. The thought of retaliation never hit when abandoned their mother. They didn't have the best relationship, but he still loved her dearly. At the moment, he knew he'd have to get them outta the ghetto, to save them from his dirt. His phone ring in this pocket getting his attention as he walked up Allied.

"Hello!" He said.

"You good?" His hype asked.

"Hell ya," he said happy to receive his first call on his trap phone.

"Where you want me to meet you?" The hype asked.

"Come to the lot we mate at." Marvell said, hoping he remembered.

"On Allied?"

"Ya I'm gone be standing out front." Marvell responded as he watched over his shoulder for an ambush.

"I'mma be there in 5 minutes." The hype said and disconnected the phone. Marvell stopped in front of his apartment building and glanced up the block noticing it was only a few people out.

He saw the hype pull in the lot, and he ran to the back of it and jumped inside.

"what you need?" He asked.

"Got $500 if you got that same shit," he said. Marvell look surprised, but quickly went in his pocket to retrieve the work. He remembered the hype thought his dimes where twentieth, so he took out 25 of them and handed it to him.

He tested one and handed over the hundred-dollar bills. Before asking Marvell what they call him.

"They call me Snake bite! What about you?" Marvell said.

"Mike"

"Aright mike, I got a deal for you. Got 2 dub for you never time you bring a friend to cop from me." Marvell said laying the foundation to get his phone knocking. Mike's eyes light up at the purposely.

"Ya that works... You keep this shit you gone have people kicking your door down." Mike said.

"Ya... It's that good?" Marvell questioned.

"Ya, that good. But I gotta get to work!" He added giving Marvell notice to get out.

"Aright don't forget two dub each person." He said opening the door and getting out. When the car exited the lot, another entered. Marvell noticed the car he broke into and reached from the dreko. But before he could pull it out someone hoped out the backseat shooting.

Bloc! Bloc! Bloc! Bloc!

Marvell ran to the side of the building for cover. He pulled the pistol and pointed around the building without look and pulled the trigger.

Boom! Boom! Boom! Boom! Boom! Boom! Boom! boom! boom!

Marvell kept firing until the clip was empty.

Too scared to go after him the shooter hoped in the back seat and the car quickly pulled out the lot.

Marvell peeked around the corner and saw he was alone before the sound of sirens was heard from all directions.

Meanwhile

Cash walked out the morgue his mind in a disarray. He just identified his mother's remains. And couldn't believe someone shot her twice in the head. Cash observed the world caving in on him. One after another everyone he treasured was dying. Why god saved him was a mystery he couldn't explain.

He made his way over to a tinted-out BMW SUV. Yangba sit behind the driver seat in two of his shooters were in the back with choppers ready for any and everything. The 20 thousand they were paid was enough compensation for a few bodies. Cash leaped inside and lay the seat back. Yangba pulled off in they roll in silence. Cash considered who was responsible for his mother's murder. There was an endless number for people who could've done it. But the one person that stuck was June. *After all these years of feeding the little nigga he pulled something like this.* Cash thought.

Yangba tapped Cash on the shoulders and passed him the blunt. He took it in hit it two hard times hoping to take the stress away. But it did nothing to ease his pain. His mother was gone, and he felt all alone in the world. Right now, he wanted to break down and cry but couldn't trust them to see him in a moment of weakness.

If he showed any emotion, any sign verbally, his protector was liable to eat him alive. He knew this, because at one point he was them, young and reckless, with no loyalty.

Cash gazed out the window and watched as they passed so many empty souls on the stress corner. People who could only dream to live the lift he did. He wondered if they thought it was all rainbows and butterflies at the top. Little did they know the saying more money more problems were true. He'd give it all up to go back to them days with nothing to eat but sugar sandwiches if he got his family back. Back then they were poor, but away seemed to have something to smile about. Here he was prosperous with a whole in his heart. It's been months since he really had something to smile about. *One last war in I'm out* he thought, as Yangba turn up Moneybagg Yo On My Soul. Lil Durk verse had him turned up now. He loved the part where he said, *I might face the east when I'm in that Rolls case I'm in cohorts with the Moe's.* Cash laughed at Yangba going crazy in the driver seat. He reminded Cash of a younger him. He was already a leader in respected amongst his kind. *One day Yangba could become the face of the city.* Cash thought.

His mind shifted back to locating June. But that wouldn't be easy, his team went to June's mamma house and she was nowhere to be found. Cash taught June everything he knew; he was long gone in wouldn't show up until it was time to put his murder game down. Cash had one way to get to him. There was this up-and-coming rapper, Big Ryan. He was a close friend of June's; they were from the same block. Big Ryan would be able to get his location but wouldn't just give it to him. So, the scheme was to kidnap him. Cash also wanted to see if he spotted the driver of the minivan amount Danjunema team, at a known clubhouse of the African kingpins, in downtown, Chicago.

"A bro when we back in Chicago pull up downtown. I gotta look into something real quick." Cash yelled over the music.

Yangba looked at him like he was crazy. "You try'na go downtown with these polls?" He asked.

"Hell ya," Cash said starring out the window. *"This nigga to much!"* Yangba thought before making a U-turn. He wasn't feeling Cash bossing him around, not even a bit. *Shit he ain't my big hommie.* He thought.

An hour later

Inside the black and red duffle bag was straight fleck. The crystal's that appeared when the white substance was moved the slightest bit was amazing and brought pear joy to his face. June placed the 10 bricks of girl on the bed. Kia's workers dropped it off 20 minutes ago. He was starting to do the math in his head. Shit was looking really good. He smiled; his plan had come together. It had been a while since he followed kia from Money house the night she had him executed. It was insane how the original plan was to have Kia hit him with some work, then kill Cash in take over the city. But when Cash appeared to turn things around for the better, he abandoned the idea. Now he was being focused out and compiled back to the original plan. Life was crazy like that at times. June was feeling good, his spirits were high, with his own plug the sky was the limit. All he needed was to avoid Cash until his money was straight. There was a knock at the door. He put the bricks in a bag and placed them under the bed. When he cast out the peephole, he saw Kutta and Bullet Row. He threw the door open "what good skud?" They both said putting their hands out to shack up. June shook them and stepped aside allowing them to enter. "Bro you know the Nigga cash got a Greenlight on you." Kutta said taking a seat." What the fuck that's about?" He added.

"Man, the nigga called my phone after somebody attempted getting him hit right. He like come to the city ASAP. But real aggressive. I let shit slide; tell the nigga I'm gone be down there as soon as I'm done taking care of a few things. The nigga get to shouting talking bout get down there or I can get done like killa!" June said.

They both screwed their face up. "That bitch as nigga killed skud?" Bullet asked. June took a deep breath," I asked him that, he said nah, but by then already called him a few pussys." June said and they both burst into laughter.

"So, when we gone get him gone?" Kutta asked, once things quieted down.

"ASAP, but for now we gone stay outta town." June responded.

Kutta felt like June was letting Cash run them outta Chicago." A bro no bull shit that shit seem lame as hell. It seems like he hoeing us." He said expressing his feelings. June shook his head, he understood where he was coming from. But that was the goon mentality, the boss mentality was to wait in strike at the right moment. "I get it bro, trust me I was thinking the same, but if we gone make it outta this war in spend this money, we gone have to think in make the best move or nothing. Cash ain't gone be easy to get our hands on, so we gone have to pay to get him killed. He gone be alert, cause he know how I get down. I wanna win but I want y'all to be here with me at the end." He said. Kutta gave it more consideration and June was right. "So, what we on until then? " he asked. June went under the bed in pulled out the bricks. "This," he said throwing them on the bed. They both stood up before Kutta went into the bag. When he opened it, a smile came to their face at the exact time. " I got a new plug in we gone push this in Beloit until we get Cash out the way." June continued. Bullet pulled one out in looked it over.

"This flake," he said.

"I know bro, this better then Cash shit." June said rubbing his fingers together.

"Let get to this money, then," Kutta said.

"Let's get something to eat first before we shoot outta Town." June said. Kutta grabbed the work off the bed and throw the bag over his shoulder.

"Nah we gone come back for that" June said, walking towards the door. Kutta put the bag back down, and they followed him out. They jumped into June Range Rover. He didn't know his way around Madison but saw a few restaurants on the street around the corner. They pulled up to the west town mall in jumped out. They were dripping with swag the moment they enter the mall all eyes were on them. June wore a white and light blue Louis Vuitton polo shirt, a lair of light blue jeans, alone with dark blue, light blue and white Louis Vuitton shoes. His bust down Patel Philippe watch was worth over 100,000 thousand dollars. June looked around and saw a lot of black woman in the mall. He knew anywhere you spotted black hoes hustlers where around the corner. His thought went to when he first took over Beloit. He went up there to commit a murder and saw an opportunity. He met Kim and the rest was history. The wheels in his brain began to turn, Madison was an even bigger city then Beloit. If he could get set up here who knew where it could lead him. That's when he noticed her walking alone, she was stunning and resembled R&B singer Kehlani. Her tattoos were amazing and filled with color.

"A I'm gone catch up to y'all," he said, walking over to her. She stared at him sideways. "Hi ma, my name June," he began to say but she walked around him like he wasn't there. This was new to him. June wasn't used to this response from women. He was accustomed to them being all over him. He turned around in caught up to her. "A shorty, I'm talking to you," he said cutting her off. She rolled her eyes at him before saying, "and I'm not talking to you!" She said, try'na step around him again. June remembered something his mom taught him, if a woman wasn't responding to one approach it was because it was the wrong one, or she was already in love. So, he switched his approach becoming more professional, and respectful.

"You know what let me apologize for my behavior. I didn't come at you like the woman you are. If you'll allow me a second chance, I'll make it up. Let me have a moment of your time you want regret it..." He said. She raised her eyebrows but didn't walk away this time. "I know you don't know me, but I couldn't just walk pass without saying something. You're beautiful but I know looks ain't the only thing that defines you. I would really love if you allowed me to take you out." He said.

She eyed him up and down. He was sexy, and his good looks in long dreadlocks made him her type. "Ion know bout that." She said. He wasn't from Madison; she grew up there and never once saw him a day in her life. June noticed the expression on her face. She was interested but uncertain on whether it would be safe. "I know what you thinking, we don't have to go nowhere we could set down in the food court, and just have a conversation over a meal. I know that ain't a good first date for my future wife, but I'm willing to do whatever to get that date." He joked. June knew he had her when she let out a light giggle. "Boy you moving too fast," she said, looking at him wondering if she should take him up on his offer. Why not she thought.

"Okay, fine." She said. June flashed a smile, knowing he had someone to show him around this town. Once he turned his charm on, she'd be all his.

* * * * * *

Marvell was lucky to escape to his sister's house after the shooting. When he got there, she wasn't home, so he let his self in with his key. Before going to take a shower and hopefully remove any gunshot residue. After getting out, he called his homie TT, and told him to slide to his sister crib it was import.

TT was there and know time, he walked inside the first thing he asked was "where yo fine as sister at."

Marvell gave him a stare that said stop playing with me. He didn't play when it came to his sister. He wanted her to find a good loving man with a job not some thug, that would dog her every chance he got.

"Bro cut the bullshit!" He said seriously.

"Man, I'm just playing with yo soft ass," TT lied. He wants her bad, and if he got the chance, he was smashing.

"But what's so important?" He asked taking a seat in the kitchen. Marvell shook his head still shocked about what happened.

"Man, it's a long story, but the short one is I hit a lick, then had to fuck the same nigga up. He came back and had some nigga shoot at me in front of my crib." He said.

TT looked at him awhile before asking one of the many questions that came to mind." You hit a lick for what?" he asked, greed his first concern.

Marvell pulled out the two pistols and the coke he came up on along with the cash. TT smiled, "okay this what I'm talking bout." He said picking up one of the polls and looking it over. "Sell me this?" He asked. Marvell looked at the other pistol. He only needed one," what you gone give me for it?" He questioned not knowing it worth. TT took advantage or is inexperience, "I got $150," he said.

"Bet," Marvell said excitingly. He was cool with getting something for the stolen property. TT went in his pocket and quickly pulled out the cash and handed it over. "You selling this work?" He asked try'na get over again.

"Nuh, I'm good. I'm gone move this on my own." Marvell responded. TT raised is eyebrows excited to see him enter the belly of the breast and get some money.

"So, what we gone do about the nigga who you pocked?" TT asked. Marvell didn't know his name, the only thing he knew was how he looked.

"Shit I don't know that's why I called you!" He said. TT thought on awhile before saying," we gotta put him down! shit, he knows where you lay yo head."

Marvell though about it, TT was right." How we gone do that?" Marvell asked.

TT laughed inside, he had just the plan....

Meanwhile

The interior of the bar was exquisite and high scale. But today it was empty except for a few customers. It was quiet, as everyone waited for a response from the man in charge. Fear was the emotion everyone in attendance felt because they failed him. Danjunema sat inside his hangout with his whole team. They closed the bar when we entered the building. The owner didn't sweat money Danjunema always spent big. Sometimes he spent what they made all month in one visit. He lit up a cigar and took a big pull, as one of his employees begin to explain how they missed the hit on Cash. It was funny to him, how he told the story. Cash was on them from the beginning. At least he wasn't slow, like Danjunema thought, when he was informed Cash was riding around solo.

He waved his hand, telling the man he'd heard enough. "It's ok shit happens. There's always next time." He said putting them all at ease. The whole room feared he'd be upset with their fairer. But he wasn't something about today had him and a good mood. He stood up and everyone in the room followed. The owner waved goodbye as they exited the building. He wasn't worried about compensation; the African was more than good for it.

Danjunema walked outside along with his team, headed to see his daughter at the hospital. Hopefully today would be the day she fought her way outta the coma. The war was going his way so far, the only thing was when they had an opportunity to kill Cash they missed. But that was war at times. They'd get another chance, and the chances of them missing twice was slim to none.

They were some of Africa best soldier, war was second nature to them.

One of his bodyguards pulled his pistol with a quickness, he hadn't saw in some time.

Boom! Boom Boom.

Shots ring out from a Passing SUV. Before Danjunema was pushed to the ground he saw Cash firing out the window. His man exchanged gunfire with Cash as he continued to fire over a hundred rounds. When the van reached the end of the block Danjunema stood to his feet. There were body's all around him. He glanced around in saw soldiers holding wounds, and bleeding out in front of him, and had a flashback of this time in the African army. The guard that saved his life stood tall against the living." We gotta go!" He said headed to the car firearms in hand. Danjunema followed them and they jumped in a number of different cars before speeding away from a bloodbath. He relaxed in his seat thankful to be alive. A smile spread across his face. His adrenaline was rushing, it reminded him of his young years. At war in Africa, but if that's all Cash had to offer then it wouldn't be much of a war. Real war took deep thought and planned out attacks. Cash killed a few bodyguards, people he could care less about. While on the other hand Danjunema took his mother. He laughed out loud as his driver look back wondering what was laughable. Danjunema just kept on laughing. Cash didn't know he was beefing with a mad man.

* * * * *

Cash set back as Yangba drove fast try'na get away from downtown as quickly as possible. He'd hit a lot of them but was sure he'd missed Danjunema. The driver of the minivan that shot at Cash pushed him to the pavement.

Even though he missed he was relieved to know who he was at war with. Now he could put a plan together to win it. But first they had to get away from this scene safe. Yangba's driving skills were the best Cash ever seen. He flew up the street with skill hitting corner, without slowing down. Before Cash knew it, they were flying up the highway. He let out a breath when they drove past the White Sox's stadium. He looked over to where the buildings used to be. It had been a long time but he still missed State way! He learned all the shit that paved the way to become a king from being raised in them buildings.

They showed him to stand on his own two feet. How friendships worked, and how that same comrade could be the death of you. He peeked over at Yangba, knowing he couldn't be trusted, but for now they would watch his back. He would pay for their services, until they were no longer needed. Once June was out the way he'd be about to trust his guys again.

They pulled up on 85th in parked the car a few houses down. Cash handed the young boy in the back his chopper back and step out without saying a word to them. He walked over to his car as they set in the SUV and jumped in. Then pulled his .40 off this hip and placed it on this lap. He started the car and pulled off. When he hit the corner, he was ambushed. Two vans blocked him in, and men jumped out wearing masks. It was like Daivo, Cash started firing shot out the windshield, while reaching for the doorknob with the opposite hand, getting out the car. The shooter ducked low but kept advancing on the vehicle. They waste gone miss like the last team.

Cash docked behind the back of the car, while they switch cheese it with bullets. He peeked his head up and fired two shot in one of their chests, he watched him fall to the pavement, before ducking back down. Two of the men split up one going to the right side on the vehicles, the to the left. Cash stuck up head to the left and fires a single shot that found a home in the man head but not before he was able to fire around that snacked Cash in the shoulder.

The other shooter came up behind him shooting him in the back knocking him face first to the ground. Cash began crowing while trying to catch his breath. Blood poured from his mouth in noise. He griped the handle of his pistol tight while giving his all to turn over and continue the fight but was unsuccessful. The shooter bent at the knees while pointing his gun at the back of Cash head. He wanted to watch as he blew his brains out. Once he was sure he was close enough that it was impossible for Cash to serve he pulled the trigger.

Bloc!

Cash's brains exploded; brain matter landed on the mask of the shooter. It reminded him of a watermelon busting and he enjoyed it more than sex.

Cash soul left his body his mother and bother came to him. They were smile for a moment. Then his mother began to cry. He wondered why as he walked to them. Money hugged her as she continued to sob. Cash didn't understand why. He began to run to them but the faster he run the farther away them became.

" You forgot to ask him to save your soul!" Money said as a lone tear escaped his eyes.

"Repent baby" His mother said but it was too late for him, his soul had already left his body. Cash felt something strong grab at his feet before for he began a free fall to hell.

Meanwhile

June and his new friend Naomi were leaving the mall headed to her car. Their meal had gone perfect, she'd fallen for him. *He had good conversation but not good enough to fuck just yet.* She thought. He wasn't going home with her but just walking her to the car. She'd giving him her number, so it was only a matter of time. When they reached her car, his phone rang. June picked it up.

"Hello" he answered. His mouth floored when his mother told him the news. He didn't know whether to be pleased or shed a tear. He put his hand over his mouth.

"You their baby?" She asked, once he didn't respond.

"Where you hear this at "he asked.

"Everybody in Chicago talking about it baby."

"When it happen?" He asked, as Naomi got in the car. She put her hand up to her ear, like a phone letting him know to call her. June shook his head ok, too focused on the announcement that Cash was dead.

"Not long-ago baby, they killed him by his car." She said. He heard sadness in her voice. He was devastated as well; they'd just lost one of the best Black Disciples since Dave. June thought even though they were at war he knew what his lost would mean to the guys. The city would morn his death...

"Damn ma," he said as Naomi pulled off. She waved as she left. He returned the gesture before saying, " Where at?"

"On 83rd, they saying them new boys he been with, might've had him killed, but that's just one of many rumors. Well that's what I think it's too early to know anything..... It sad because his mother was killed the day before as well." She said pausing to let him speak. He was lost for word; his mind was unsettled at the moment. He'd began to see Cash as untouchable after all he'd been through. Now he was gone. "Somebody killed Ms. Moore to?" He asked his voice cracking. Ms. Moore was a good person; she didn't deserve what happened to her.

"Ya baby they shot her dead while she sleep." His mother responded. At that moment June made a promise no one would ever see his mother again. He was moving her fare away from everything he did.

"Ok ma, I love you. I want you to find somewhere nice to move pick a new state somewhere safe. Then find a house, I'm gone buy it for you." He said walking back towards the mall. Kutta and Bullet exited it smiling hard as hell. "Bro I know you heard the news, that bitch ass nigga got murked?" Kutta asked. June shook his head yes. They both look at him confused unable to understand why he appeared sad to them.

"Find something ASAP ma. I don't want you going back down there," he said.

"OK baby"

"Love you" he said before disconnecting the line.

"You good skud? Why you looking like that?" Bullet asked. June thumbed his nose before saying, "I got mixed emotions right now. Its good and bad he gone. Even though, he was gone have to go, I'm sad to see him gone. He represented a lot for us," June said. Referring to the gang his words hit them like a ton of bricks.

"Damn I never thought about that." Kutta said knowing they'd just lost someone important.

"Ya this shit fucked up!" June said walking to the car. They all got in and pulled off. It was quiet until June said, "I want ya to go back to the city. I'm gone see what's up down here for a while. Y'all can take 5 of them moves down there to. When y'all down there check in with the guys and see what the word is on who killed Cash. Make sure my name ain't mentioned in that shit." He said, as the pulled up to his hotel.

"Say know mo skud!" Kutta said as Bullet got out to go grab the work. They walked to the room together bullet was talking but June wasn't paying him any attention. He was to occupied thinking, it felt like the next 5 minutes, passed by without him being in his own body. He saw Bullet get the coke in leave, but not through his own eyes. When he sat back on the bed, he closed his eyes and memories of him, and Cash went through his mind.

"Damn, RIP Bro." He said out loud.

June lay there with his eyes close letting the day's events seep into his thoughts. He'd just been put in position to take over Chicago, and maybe even discovered a new stomping ground, only time would tell. He picked up the phone and called Black.

"Hello," she answered.

"I'm coming to get you in the morning." He said with a smile on his face. He understood why Black thought he'd abandoned her when he left. But that was the last thing on his mind. He just wanted to keep her safe. Now that Cash was gone, he didn't have to worry about her wellbeing.

"Okay boy get here soon. I'm bored outta my mind." She said thankful he was safe. Since he'd been gone, all she'd done was daydream about the kiss they shared. Her feelings were a little hurt when he rushed out leaving her horny.

"Don't trip I'm leaving out first thing in the Am." He said.

"Don't send me off cause I can't be alone tomorrow." She said with a sudden sadness in her voice. June heard the change in tone. "What's happening tomorrow." He questioned. There was a pause on the phone, as Black debated whether to tell him or not.

"Tomorrow is my birthday." She finally said.

"Say know mo. I'm gone be there no bullshit..." He said. Joy filled his voice. "How old you turning? " he added before she was able to respond. They'd discussed a lot over the last three months, but her age wasn't one of them! June assumed she was around his age.

"18" she whispered, placing her hands over her face. June was stunned, she didn't seem underage. Her demeanor was that of a grown woman. She was cool under pressure, didn't play too much, and comprehended when to ask questions, and when to leave something alone. He didn't want to make her any more uncomfortable than she already seemed, so he left it alone.

"So, we gotta turn all the way up then!" He said.

"And you know this man!" Black said doing her best impression of Smokey from Friday. June laughed at her. She was her own person. He noticed she was becoming comfortable.

"Yo ass crazy" he said.

"I ain't crazy, I'm insane!" She said using an inside joke between her in her friends. It was at that instant she realized she'd be spending her first birthday without them in years.

"Naw you ain't insane, you just faking" he joked. Getting outta the bed. He wanted to surprise her tonight. He grabbed his car keys before looking in the mirror.

"Boy whatever just make sure you come see me tomorrow." She said. June stared at his self a moment longer before walking out the door. "I got you, no lie I'm gone see you tomorrow" he lied ending the conversation. The second he was off the phone with Black he picked made another call to get her a gift.

* * * * * *

There was a slight breeze, and a hype strolling down the block penniless and in search of a come up. But he wasn't the only person on Allied Dr. searching for trouble.

A black Oldsmobile sat in the parking lot waiting on the young boy to exit the building again to steal his soul. The man Marvell robbed held his .40 and his right hand and a blunt and his left. His shooter sat behind the wheel, setting his one out as the triggermen. His big homie wanted to get his hands dirty for once which he was cool with. He'd come to view him as a pussy, and wanted to see, if he had it and him to body something.

"I can't wait to blow this lil nigga head off." He said geeking his self-up. The shooter shook his hand up and down. But still unable to believe him. "As soon as this pussy walk back outta that building," he added just as Marvell exited putting something in his pocket and strolling away from the building.

"There he go right there," the shooter said louder than necessary from excitement. The guy with the pistol sat quiet, allow Marvell to move always from the door before he stepped out. Marvell back was to him and the young shooter watched from the car as his big homie stuck up behind his unsuspecting victim. Excitement came over him as vision of seeing someone get their brain blow out was so close.

But what happened next made him reach for his pistol, but no matter how quickly he moved he'd never get there in time. A man in all black with a black T-shirt over his face appeared from thin air out the brushes. Just as his big homie raised his pistol to fire a kill shot, one was delivered on him from behind.

Bloc!

He never saw it coming, when his body dropped Marvell turned around and stood over him apparently unfazed, by the gun shot and pulled out his pistol while he stood next to the masked man and shot the dead body a few times before they ran off together. The shooter and the car were too late and slowly got out the vehicle and walked over to the homie and shock. When he was close enough to see him, what was left of his head caused him to gag. There was no question he was gone.

Hour later

Kia walked in the house her pussy sore. The beating June gave her earlier was something insane. But she loved every moment of it. After fucking him she went to see her friends at the trap on Allied. They spent the day laughing and enjoying each other's company. They even joked about the time they got caught stealing from Danjunema store back in the day. That shit seemed like a lifetime ago. Kia left after hearing shots, and on her ride home she learned there was a murder just down the street.

Kia placed her bag on the bed before walking into the rest room to take a shower. She'd spent the day with a funky pussy, too busy to come home in shower. Shit she thanked god her husband wasn't home, she laughed at herself for being so reckless. What if he wanted to fuck the second she walked through the door. It was dumb but something about the risk excited her. She began to undress, her mind still on the long poll she'd discovered. *They would be fucking real soon* she thought. Before she stepped in the shower the bathroom door came open. Danjunema walked in on her as she got in.

"How you doing daddy? " she asked noticing dirt on his shirt.

"A lot has happened today. I was shot at downtown. And I lost some more guard." He said leaning back on the sink.

He'd spent all day waiting to get home to his wife to vent. They always told each other about their day in the Streets. It was one of the best things about having a partner in the game.

"Who shot at you daddy?" She asked concerned.

"Cash! You know the man I told you about. The one that runs the Black Disciples." He said.

Kia new who he was talking about more then he'd even know. Danjunema had money killed but never once laid eyes on him. So, he had no idea Cash was his twin brother and Kia didn't see a reason for telling him.

"He tried to kill me!" He said laughing." And now he dead. My soldier got him a few minutes later." He said with a straight face. Kia glared at him and saw Satan in his eyes. He was a man on a different level. She believed it was only a matter of time before Cash was dead once she learned he had hostilities with

Danjunema. She wanted him killed anyway for the way he did his twin. Even though she had him cut down she'd never forget how Cash talked down to Money in her presents. Kia smiled at her husband happy he'd completed his objective and came out victorious.

"That's good baby it's one less thing to worry about." She said turning the water on. Danjunema watched as the water run over her body, his wife was something to behold. She was a sight to see. "Stop starring daddy you making me uncomfortable" she said. He was eyeing her like a piece of meat." If you ain't gone join me, the least you can do is wash my back." She added turning to give him a better view of her ass.

It was tempting but he had business to attend to. "I can't right now. I got to make a few calls. There might be some blowback behind what I just did. I need to put my people in position for war," he said.

"Ok daddy" Kia said, putting her head under the watch. Danjunema took this as a sign to leave. Kia was glad he didn't take her offer. Her cat was sore anyways. She took the next 20 minutes to shower before stepping out and drying off. When she came out, she saw her husband was gone. She noticed he'd forgotten his phone. Kia picked it up and went through it. She didn't know why but something inside told her to. When she made it to his picture there was a lot of photos of a cute young woman. Some with a few other women and other of her lying unconscious in a hospital bed. She heard his keys and the front door, and quickly placed his phone down. Her husband walked in and gave her a kiss before grabbing his phone.

"I'll see you later baby" he said. Kia didn't respond, she had to many questions.

"Who is that in your phone?" She finally asked. Danjunema looked at her baffled. "What?" He questioned.

"The bitch in the hospital bed?" She yelled, her emotions getting the best of her.

"Don't call her that!" He responded.

"Fuck you mean, don't call her that?" She asked folding her arms over her chest.

"It ain't what it look lik-"

"Then what is it?" She asked cutting him off, while biting her bottom lip.

"That's our child" he answered. Kia mouth fell open. She put her hand out for the phone and he handed it to her. She glimpsed at the girl as tears run down her face. She had even more questions than before. How did he know? How had he found her? Why was she in the hospital? All thing she planned on asking when she found the words.

Meanwhile

June knocked on the hotels door the moment it turned 12:00am. He'd spent the last 10 minutes outside waiting until it did. When Black opened it, she looked like she'd falling asleep.

"You wasn't supposed to come until tomorrow!" she said, stepping aside to let him in. June walked in holding a bottle of Hennessey.

"Well I'm here now" he said walking pass her in going to the bathroom to take a piss. He put the bottle down on the sink, pulled his dick out without closing the door. When Black walked by she saw it and her mouth watered. *Damn* she thought. Walking back over and taking a seat on the bed. She wanted him badly, and tonight she was gone to have her wish. June took a piss and wished his hands afterwards. He grabbed the bottle and handed it to Black.

"Boy, what's this? I ain't fucking with you..."

"Man the party starting right now." He said going in his pocket and pulling out a box. "Here, happy birthday," he added. Black took the box and open it. Inside was a diamond bracelet. She stood up, and gave him a hug, "thank you!" She said holding him tight. She pressed herself up against his hard body. June pulled away, filling his dick start to stiffen. Black pulled him back to her." June, I want this bad. I know how you feel, about us. But trust me when I say you ain't forcing me to do nothing I don't want." She said getting on her tiptoes placing a soft kiss on his lips.

June tried to fight the urge inside but couldn't. Black was amazing looking and had a great personality.

"You sure?" He asked.

"Yes" she moaned, placing her hand on his dick. She stepped back and began to unbutton his pants. June watched as she pulled them down to his knees. His dick sprang forward, and she took it with both hands stroking it until it was nice in hard. She stared into his eyes the whole time. June licked his lips seductively casing her pussy to tingle. "I want you to fuck me good! It been too long since I had some dick so take yo time" she said stepping back in undressing. When she was naked June slowly laid her back on the bed. He took his clothing all the way off before getting between her legs. Black appeared nervous when he grabbed ahold of his long poll and smack her clit with it. He did this a few times, casing her pussy to tingle each time. June placed a kiss on her lips before slowly putting the head inside. She was so tight he had to regroup. Black let out a moan from deep within. He sucked on her lip as he placed more of his cock inside her. It felt so good being taking after all these months. She was going crazy. His touch was nice in slow. June took his time he wanted to make the moment memorable for her.

He pulled all the way out and pushed back in cautiously but forceful. She couldn't believe a dick could go so deep. It felt like he was in her stomach. June looked down and saw lust in her eye.

"Damn June, fuck meee gooood!" She whispered in his ear.

"Turn around." He said pulling out. Black was disappointed when he pulled out." It's too big to let you fuck from the back," she protested.

"I know what I'm doing. I ain't gone hurt you," he said leaning down placing a kiss on her lips and helping her up. Black got up and put her ass in the ass. He got on his knees and licked her asshole. Taking her by surprise, she jumped and tried to run but her grabbed her hips pulling her back.

"That feel toooo gooddddd" she yelled. He licked her ass and played with her pussy from behind for 5 minutes before standing up and placing the head of his dick inside her again. Black had in orgasm instantly. June took a hold of her ass cheeks and began to fuck her nice and slow. After a few minutes she began to throw her as back at him wanting him to fuck her harder. Just stopped stroking and allowed her to take control. Black began to make her ass slap against him hard as she took his whole poll inside.

"Ya, throw that ass back!" June said loving how she felt.

"You like that?" she asked.

"Hell ya" he said filling his nut coming. Black felt his dick swell inside her and knew what was coming. She began to throw it back even Harder. June put his hands on her hips and pounded her. Black began to run but he held on tight blowing a big load inside her. She fell into her stomach as he lay on her back his dick still inside. June placed kisses over her shoulders as they caught their breath.

"Happy birthday," he joked.

"Thank you" black said thankful for the gift he'd just giving her.

Kia mind was blown after hearing everything her husband told her. She learned how he found out about their child, and how long he knew. He also told her about the murders their daughter committed, and how she tried to kill Cash. The part that broke her heart, was that she almost lost her life.

Kia was so ashamed of herself at that instant. She felt like less of a woman and couldn't even look her husband in the eyes. They sat at the dining room table in silence.

"Kia why didn't you just come to me? I would've done any and everything for you. I would have giving you the world. You could have come to me..." He said.

Kia looked up, at him in saw the pain in his eyes. "You don't get how I felt at the time. I had just lost my virginity to someone I didn't choose. I hated you at that time. I didn't trust you. This decision was tough on me. I cried for mouths. Felt sick to my stomach, I hated myself for this. I push this thought so deep in the back of my mind, that I made myself forget I had a child. She said tearing up. Danjunema looked at her, as she broke down putting her face into her hands. He walked over and hugged her.

"I know our pass isn't the best, but our future is what we make it." He said.

Kia held him tight wishing she'd been stronger, wishing she'd watched over her baby. Now look where they were! Their daughter had been in the hospital for months. She wasn't a girl but a cold-hearted killer like her parents.

"I need to see my baby!" She said, wanting to look at her child and say a prayer over her. She wanted to ask god to take her and give their child another chance at life.

Chapter Three

* * * * *

June woke up with black in his arms. They'd fucked until the wee hours of the night. He looked over at her as she slept, *I hope this don't make thing change.* He thought. Sex had its way of fucking up friendships. Most women thought because they shared their body with you you had to love them in return.

June liked black but he wasn't looking to be in a relationship. His heart was still with Kim and he wasn't ready to replace her with a soul just yet. He wanted to hold on to her memory just a little longer.

Black opened her eyes and noticed him starring at her. She smiled before getting outta bed to take a shower.

June wondered what was going through her mind. He would ask later, but for now he wanted to let her enjoy her birthday. June stood up and picked up the phone book. He looked through it until he found a 5-star restaurant. He called in got them a reservation, for tonight. 20 minutes later Black came out the bathroom in just a towel, he was laid back on the bed smoking a built.

She took a seat next to him, and he passed her the built. She pulled her locks to the side and took a big pull before passing it back.

"June, last night was wonderful." She said looking him in his eyes, "But that's last night. I don't want nothing from you, or I don't want to be with you. I just want you to touch that spot for me when I need it." She said, hoping she didn't offend him.

June smiled, before sitting up in placing a peck on her lips. "That works for me."

Black smiled, happy they had an understanding. She didn't want to be with a man that fine they were always trouble and came with a flock of woman. She wasn't insecure at all, but she wasn't dumb. He wouldn't be breaking her heart.

"Why don't you get dress ma, so we can turn up for your day. I know you ain't try'na be cooped up in this room." he said.

Black jumped up and went to retrieve her bags. She threw them on the bed and found something to wear before going back to the bathroom to dress. When she stepped out 20 minutes later, she looked amazing. June starred at her; he was stunned at how her locks flowed down her chest to the middle of her stomach. She'd braided them the day before and took them down, so they crouch up.

"Damn shorty you look good." He said, unable to take his eyes off her. Black stood there a moment just letting him peep swag, before saying "thank you," and, walking to look in the mirror. June got up and came behind her pulling her close. This a good look he said as he held her. Black looked them over they did look good together, but she wasn't on that with him.

June noticed she was uncomfortable with his statement and wanted to ease her mind. "I'm fucking with you black" he said smiling. Black let out a deep breathe, "thank god! " she said, "I thought you let the pussy get the best of you!" She joked, and they both laughed. June released her and walked to the bathroom. He turned around and took one last look at her ass, grabbed his bag, and went to take a shower.

* * * * *

Marvell stared in the mirror holding a stack of cash in a pistol, getting ready to go on Facebook live. He wanted to show everybody he was out here getting money. He smiled at the clout he was gone receive once the girls saw him flexing.

He put the pistol down and went live, "ya this yo boy snake bite," he said throwing up his set. "I'm out here, for all y'all opps niggaz who want smoke roll up," he said holding put the dreko he sold TT yesterday. "We ain't doing know lacking!" He said shacking his dreadlocks while pointing the pistol at the screen. "Got that shit to get a nigga mind right," he added, before putting the gun down and pulling out the cash and holding it up. "plus, we getting money pussy, nigga fuck with the snacks get bite." He said as TT walking into the camera view.

"Ya the tees, ain't fucking around nigga know how TT get down." TT added while going in his pocket and pulling out 30,000 making the 5 Marvell had look light. "On MC it, TT in the cut a scary sight!" Marvell said as they laughed about the murder before signing off. TT walked out the bathroom in into Marvell's sister living room. She wasn't at home which was a letdown to him cause he was looking forward to see that fat ass. Marvell came out as TT pick up his lean and took a sip.

"A TT why you be fucking with that bullshit?" Marvell asked against drug use.

"What bullshit?" TT asked already knowing what he was talking about.

"Man, you know!" He said point at the dibble coup.

"Come on tee, I ain't gone keep doing his with you. I fuck with it cause I want. " TT said getting defensive. Marvell let it go cause there was no changing TT mind on the subject. He just hated to see him abusing drugs like they weren't addictive. He sat down and let it go, while going on Facebook. He had a few inbox messages and looked them over a couple from some of the snacks asking him who he was into it with which he skipped over. He saw a couple females who was on some sack chasing shit, but it didn't stop him from responding to them. Once he started a few different conversations with them he turned his attention to TT. Who was on the arm of the couch.

"A tee, you my nigga." he said. TT looked at him questionably. "Fuck you on tee," he asked. Marvell stood up playing last night events in his head.

"Bro you bust that boy brain like it was nothing." He said animatedly. TT laughed, "it wasn't tee!" He said taking another sip, before adding." So, you hustling now?" He asked switching the topic.

"Hell ya," Marvell said.

"Say no mo when you run outta that work I could get you some mo make sure you fuck with me tee." TT said, standing to his feet to leave. "I'm outta here bro" he said.

"I got you Tee when this move gone I'm gone reup from you." Marvell said walking him to the door and locking it behind him. Once he was along, he turned up some music and grabbed the dreko and went back to the mirror to admire himself some more. But his self-made video shoot didn't last long as he received a call one his trap phone.

"Who!" He asked.

"Where you want me to meet you?" Mike asked.

"Pull over on Carline," he said.

"Ok be there soon! I'll call once I'm on that block" Mike said. And they hung up the phone Marvell was happy more money was coming in. He continued making his video for another 20 minutes before Mike called back.

Marvell went outside and got in the back seat of Mikes cars because there was a white woman on the passage side.

"What you need?" he asked ASAP.

"We got a thousand, Mike said but only if you got the same move." Mike said.

"I do Mike, damn," Marvell said sick of the same question. He went and his bag and got the work for them before handing it to Mike who looked at it and noticed it was the same. Before handing him the money. The lady looked back saying, "can I get yo number?" handing him her phone. Mike looked at her upset, but this didn't stop her. Marvell put his number and her phone and pushed call for he could get hers as well. Before handing it back to her and stepping out the car. *Another customer* he thought walking back to his building.

* * * * *

The air was cold in the hospital from the air-conditioning. Everyone seemed to be moving slow without a care in the world. But things seem to fly but as Kia walked with a sense of urgency, unable to slow her legs down. She rushed to Bee's room. When she saw her baby girl with all the machines hook up to her, she began to weep. She strolled closer and looked into her child's beautiful face. They looked so much alike. Bee was a spitting image of her when she was young. Kia placed her hand on Bee arm and rubbed it lightly. "I'm so sorry baby!" She whispered. "I know you probably hate me," she added taking a seat in the chair next to the bed. "I was weak, and didn't know what to do," she continued as the tears began to poor from her eye's. Kia sealed her eyes to stop them, placing her head on the bed next. Today was a new low for her, never once had she been this emotional destroyed. Just seeing the aftermath of the abandonment of her child took her soul way. Kia stood to her feet, she had to get outta there before she fell into a deep, deadly depression. But before she could walk away, she placed a kiss on Bee's forehead. "I'm so sorry, baby... I know it might not seem like it, but momma loves you dearly." She said walking out the room. Bee opened her eyes the instant the strange woman left the room. She was so disorient. She'd awoken from the coma just moments before the lady walked in, but outta fear she was pretending to still be comatose. Bee seat there as here memory began to return. She remembered the night she was shot, the Africans saving her, and Martez friend being the shooter. Bee laughed at the thoughts of that night it was a set up from the beginning. Martez wasn't a fool like she thought. But if he thought this was over, he had another thing coming. She wouldn't stop until she had his blood on her hands.

Kia walked back into the hospital room to retrieve her purse and Bee was seated up in bed. Her heart dropped as she starred at her baby girl. Bee sat there unable to find words. There were so many questions she needed answered but didn't know where to begin. Apart of her despised her parents, but the child inside always wanted a real family. Not one put together at a foster home. Kia slowly walked over to the bed; she was a mess. The tears wouldn't stop pouring.

"Can I help you?" Bee brought herself to say, unable to admit this was her mother. Kia couldn't bring herself to speak. What could she say to explain the betrayal of leaving. There was no explanation good enough for what she'd done.

"Do I know you?" Bee questioned.

"I'm...I'm... Your mother." She finally managed to spit it out.

"I don't have a mother." Bee said as tears began to wheel up in her eyes. She'd waited her whole life for this moment, and now that it was here, she didn't know if she could forgive. She'd learn to forget, and gotten past the feeling of not being wanted, but not those emotion came rushing back. She was that frighten child in a foster home once again. Mind racing inquiring whether she was good enough to love. Who would ever love a child who parents wouldn't love them? Why had they left??? A tear fell from her eyes as the emotions and anger mixed with sadness overwhelmed her.

"I would feel the same way if I was you.... But you do have a mother. I know I fuc-"

"Look bitch, I ain't got no mother like I said. So, you can get the fuck out!" Bee said the resentment getting the best of her. For a microsecond Bee wished she had her savages, to put her down, for trying to walk back in her life, like she never abandoned her. Kia looked at the pain in her child eyes and wouldn't give up this time. She believed they needed each other. "I know you mad but I ain't going know where without you... I made that mistake before, and I'm damn shore not gone make it twice. I was a child myself and didn't know how to stand on my decisions. But now I'm a woman and I want you to let me make this up to you." Kia pleaded.

"How the fuck you gone do that?" Bee yelled.

"Just come with me. We can talk, I could help you with so much."

"I don't need yo help with shit!" Bee said.

"I talked to your father, and learn what you've been up to, for the last few months. I see you got some hustle inside. I could get you any product you desire in assist you with getting revenge on the person who put you in the hospital." Kia said, with a smirk on her face. This got Bee attention. "Any product?" She asked.

"Yes!" Kia said putting her hand out to help her outta the bed.

* * * * *

"I got this for you," June said handing Black a diamond necklace over the table. Black opened the box and saw the necklace; it was beautiful. She looked up at June as she smiled. She was speechless, the second gift was unexpected. June looked at the joy in her eyes and the 15 bands he'd spent was worth it. "You didn't have to!" Black said once she found her voice. June laughed, out loud. "I know I ain't have to... I did it cause I wanted to..." He said still laughing. "I know we met fucked up so I wanted to use this moment to say I'm sorry. I was just going through a lot that day. I lost the love of my life and was taking my pain out on any and everyone. I hope you can forgive me."

"I do, it's water until the bridge..." She said. June did some fucked up things the day she met him, but since then he'd been nothing but a gentleman. It was strange but she forgotten how they met for the most part. All she noticed when she saw him was a friend, something to hold on to while alone in the world, anything else didn't matter. June stood up and strolled over to her, he took the necklace from the box and place it on her neck. Making sure to rub her shoulders. Black loved his touch and closed her eyes.

"Happy birthday!" He whispered in her ear, before taking his seat.

"Thank you so much, I thought I was gone spend the day alone. It means so much that you came to celebrate with me," she said securely.

They finished their meal, before heading back to the hotel for the night. When they walked into the room, they were both tipsy and feeling good. June fell on the bed and closed his eyes. Black climbed on top of him. She was horny as hell and planed on getting fucked again long and hard for the night. She just hope he was up for the challenge. She began to place kiss over over his neck and rub his long dick through his pants. June laid there feeling his liquor. "I want to fuck!" She whispered.

"I can see that" he said putting his arms around her pulling her closer. "You know this dick like heroin, you could get hooked." He warned.

"Ain't nobody gone get hook, I just want it for the night." She said, looking into his eyes. "Then get what you want. But if you gone do this dick do it right." He said. With that said black stood up and unzipped his pants, she pulled his half hard cock from them and began to stroke him. June watched as his member grew.

"Damn that feels good." He said.

"This gone feel even better," she said bending at the waste and putting him and her mouth. She slowly sucked him while moving her tongue back and forth over his cock. She let spit run down to his balls before she began to use both hands to stroke his dick. Making sure to stop and rub his balls as well. June couldn't take it anymore and decided to return the favor. He pulled his dick outta her mouth and rubbed it over her face. Then stood up and undressed her. He told her to get on all fours, once she assumed the position, he undressed himself before dropping to his knees and attacking her asshole with this tongue from the back. Black let out a scream of pleasure before pushing back against him.

"Shiiiit, that's feels good." She said. June opened her ass cheek to get deeper inside licking her from her pussy up over and over driving her crazy. June spent the rest of the night making sure to give black the best birthday ever.

Chapter Four

* * * * *

"Why the fuck would you tell our baby something so fuck crazy?" Danjunema yelled at Kia in their bedroom. Bee listened to them clashing for the last hour. Her father seemed really upset at her mother for telling her she'd supply her with drugs. "I did know what else to say." Kia whispered. She had concerns with her actions as well in Danjunema wasn't doing anything to make her feel better.

He looked at his wife sitting on the bed with her head down. She was confused and hurt. He could see it on her face. It wasn't helping for him to jump down her throat. He took a seat next to her and hugged her, Kia broke down in his arms." I... I ... I didn't know what else to say." She cried. "I know but we can't give her drugs... " he responded. Kia pulled away from him and stared in his eyes with desperation, "we have to, I can't lie to her now She'll never trust me." Kia said. Danjunema gazed into his wife eyes, and the look in them tormented him. "Damn it Kia," he said as the thought of letting his only child become a drug pusher ran through his mind." If I do this, she has to learn everything from me personal. That's the only way I will allow this." He said. Kia face lit up, "Ok I'll go tell her," Kia said standing to leave the room.

Bee rushed back down the hallway into the room she was assigned. She would be staying with them and their mansion in Chicago until further notice... Her mother wouldn't let her leave her side, so she'd retrieve her things from Madison later. She thought about Martez and how he tried having her killed. Even though she was there to murder him, she still felt betrayed and some weird way. Since she awoken, he was all she thought about. The love they shared would never fade, but there was no forgiving the slugs he had put in her. She planned to kill him herself if it was the last thing she never did.

Kia walked in the room interrupting her thought. She looked at her mother, and couldn't help noticing how much they resembled. Kia had cleaned herself up and there was no sign of the tears she'd just shed a moment ago.

"Your father said it's ok. But you have to learn everything from him." Bee just shook her head yes. She was more than willing to have a mentor in the game. Kia spent over and hour telling kia everything about her pass in her Fathers as well. The only thing she removed was the rape. Not wanting to display her husband in negative light to their child. When she was done, Bee sat their mouth opened, amazed. Now it all made sense. The way the hustling came naturally to her, it was in her blood too.

"Why you never came looking for me." Bee asked changing the subject. Kia casted in her eye, "baby there more to this story then I can tell you. Just know I went through a lot leading up to having you. I was put out on the streets amongst other things. I just didn't know what to do and was so disappointed in myself I lied so long that I started to believe it.... I'm so sorry and I know I can't make up for it, but I will spend the rest of my life trying." Kia said from the bottom of her heart. Bee gave her a hug, the first embrace amongst mother and child, and to Kia it was heavily. "It's ok we can forget about the pass and focus on the future," Bee said holding her tight. "Now I'm gone get to know my father" she added standing to her feet. "Ok let go!" Kia said, happy to begin building a relationship.

* * * * * *

Martez was laid back in bed with is eyes closed, as he received head from two women at the same time. One was licking his balls while the other sucked on the head. Any other man would've been consumed by the pressure, but his mind was elsewhere. He'd received a call from his private investigator that Bee was out the hospital. It was only a matter of time before she'd be coming for his soul. But he'd see her coming long before she arrived. After getting the news she'd woken up, he told the PI to keep an eye on her at all times. He was aware of her whereabouts, and could have her killed.

Martez opened his eyes when the girls began to tongue kiss around the head of his cock. It was a beautiful sight. But one he couldn't truly enjoy at the moment. There was too much on his mind with bee waking up and Cash murder he just didn't feel comfortable enjoying much of anything. He pulled his dick away from them and waved them off. They appeared disappointed, but he could care less. Once he was alone, he placed his tool back inside his briefs, and stood to his feet.

Cash was his only customer and with him gone Martez was now able to walk away from the game. He was damaged about Cash, but it was a miracle he'd lasted this long. Cash played the game with everything he had, and when your all-in, it's only a matter of time before it consumed you. He would miss him, but wouldn't lose no sleep over something, he saw coming from afar. But Bee being woke had him restless, and worried. She was a threat, and as long as she was breathing, he'd have to say on point. *Damn* he was hoping she'd just pass away. When he heard that Reese was dead, and that Bee served, his heart dropped. It angered him he'd lost his mentor and moving on from the lost would take a lifetime. Over the last few months, he wondered what went wrong? How was Bee able to murder Reese in an ambush? He knew he'd never know what took place unless he got the story from the horse's mouth. Bee was the only person that knew what happened that dark night, or so he thought. He had no notion that she'd been saved by some of Africa's finest. Reese didn't stand a chance. Unable to sleep Martez got outta bed and got dress to take a quick trip to the store hoping the ride would take his brain off things.

* * * * *

"You said you could get anything done without a problem, and without getting your hands dirty?" Bee asked with raise eyebrows. Danjunema saw the evil in his child's eyes and knew just what she had in mind. This would be a good teaching experience. So, he smiled, before saying, "anything! What you got in mind?" He asked. Kia sat there just watching them. She really enjoyed having her whole family together. It was a dream come true. "I got murder on my mind!" Bee said, taking a deep breath. She hoped she wasn't moving too fast. "I know that but who? Just give me a name, and I'll have it done by the morning." Danjunema said.

"By the morning?" Bee asked surprised.

"Ya, murder is nothing for my man. They kill for fun back home." He said shrugging his shoulders. Bee sat and thought for a moment. This was a lot to take in, when she went in the coma, she was alone in this world. with no family or friends. Now here she was in a mansion with her parents and they were a queen pin and a kingpin. This shit was over the top and felt like a fantasy. She was also pondering the thought of having Martez killed. It was hard to think or letting somebody else put in her work, but over the last hour her father taught her the game. He enrolled her in street 101 and she learned a lot in that little time. He was right, why through bricks at the penitentiary when someone else will do it for you. Apart of her want to see if her dad was the person he claimed to be. She wasn't the type to just take a person word, actions spoke louder. She picked up a pin and wrote Martez name and address down and gave the piece of paper to him.

"I'm a little sleepy, I'll see you guys in the morning." She said turning to leave the room.

"Are you sure you want this done?" Danjunema asked giving her a chance to back out. Bee laughed inside, *this old nigga was just talking out his ass,* she thought. Bee wanted to test him and see if he was a man of his word. "Yea, I'm sure!" She said, walking out the room without looking back. Bee went to her room and glanced around; it was the size of a small apartment. She wondered if her father would come through, or if he was just a man of too many words.

Either way Martez would be dead soon, *there was no way around that*, she thought, while locking the door still a little uncomfortable around the strangers who were her parents. She laughed at the thought, life really was a rollercoaster.

* * * * *

Martez got outta his car after spending the last few hours riding around trying to clear his mind. He'd thought long and hard and would put the hit on Bee first thing in the morning. Life was too short to spend it looking over your shoulders, and that's what he'd be doing as long as his crazy ex was on this earth. He hit the lock on the key fob and walked to the door. When he opened it the house was pitch black.

He entered with caution, and reached for his firearm at his side, but found nothing, *damn*, he thought. He cursed his self for leaving without it. He made his way up the stairs, and down the hallway searching for his companions. When he entered the bedroom, his heart dropped at the sight of the woman's decapitated head laying on his bed. The room looked like a scene outta a scary movie. Martez through up on himself as he backed away from the unbelievable sight. He grabbed his mouth in shock, and all his years in the game this was the most gruesome murder scene he'd experience. It was at that moment he was broken from his thoughts, when he heard something downstairs, it was a cold, long hard laugh. It sent chills down his spine. He rushed back in the room and grabbed his 9.mm pistol, it made him feel a little safer. But the sight at the end of the hall almost caused him to relieve his bows. There was over 20 Yellow cat like eyes coming up the stairs. The sight was like lions in the Africa bush, late night hunting. He took a deep breath, knowing this was his last moment, but he was gone take a stand and fight like a man. He stood up and open fire.

BOC! BOC! BOC! BOC!

Martez stopped firing, when he noticed nothing was there. *Where they go*, he thought, as he felt cold steal at the back on his head. "Put the gun down!" A female voice said. Martez shook his head no, if he was gone die it would be a fight. The rest of the Africa come from their spot and walk towards him." I said put the gun down." The woman repeated. Martez quickly turned around and tried grabbing the pistol, but the woman backed up with a quickness and shot him and the stomach knocking him to his knees. He tried to point his pistol, but she kicked it outta his hand all in one motion. The pain in his stomach caused him to double over. Two of the Africans grabbed him but the arms and pulled him to his feet. Another one placed him in a headlock. Martez open his eyes in before him stood a beautiful light skin African woman. She was stunning with a pair of contacts lens in her eyes that resembled cat eyes. "What the fuck all y'all want!" He asked hoping to buy his way outta the situation. The woman pulled at long blade from a hoister and whipped blood from the blade. "I could pay y'all whatever to let me go just name the price." He said making one last plea, but a part of him believed this was the end. The woman strolled close in starred into his eyes a moment before plugin the knife into his neck. Martez struggle try'na pull always but his only caused the knife to go deeper. Blood poured from the wound, as his body got weak until he passed out. "We come to collect you head," the woman said as his body fell to the pavement. She pulled the knife from his neck and handed it to a man. "Cut is head off the boss want to show it to his daughter." She said licking the blood off her finger and walking out the room.

Chapter Five

* * * * *

(The next day)

The sunshine through the windshield, making it hard to see, June pulled the sun visor down to shield his eyes and cast out the window. The cornfield went on for miles, which made the ride boring. June need corners and turns to keep him alert. But today was different, he was on the expressway headed to Madison. He woke up bright at dawn and hit the streets. He was feeling solid today and wanted to begin building his new empire. He picked up the phone and called Naomi, to set up a date. She answered on the second ring, "Who is this!" She said sounding upset. June smiled cause he treasured a no nonsense woman. "This June we mate at the mall," he said hoping she remember him. He pushed the thought of being forgotten outta his mind, he was rememberable, no questions asked. Swag like his was hard to find. "Oh, ya how are you?" She asked seeming friendlier.

"I'm cooling, just was on my way in town in you came to mind." He said. Picking up his blunt and lighting it up, before putting the phone one speaker. "What came to mind about me? "she asked try'na give him a hard time." I just want to see you that's all... It would be nice to get to know you." He said. There was a giggle on the other end of the phone, and June wondered what was funny.

"How you know it would be nice, I could be the crazy type of bitch that call the police on you. Or, I could be the bitch, who fuck you have a baby, to force you to be with me." She said. June couldn't help but laugh at this, she was something else. " look ma, I got good judgement, I didn't get nothing like that from you. I saw a lot more then that type of T.H.O.T shit.... So, like I said, it would be nice to get to know you. So, is you gone give me a shot?" He questioned taking a pull of smoke that made him cough. "Boy don't smoke it if you can't handle it!" She joked. "But ya you can get to know me, just let me know when you ready" she added.

"I'm ready now! Shit to keep it real you the reasons I'm coming down there." He said.

"Who you think I am one of these goofy lil hoes, that believe everything they hear?" She asked, a little affined he was coming at her like that. June heard the change of tone in her voice, and wanted to laugh but didn't, instead he laid it on thick." No bullshit, I ain't lying, I don't know a soul down there. " he said exiting the highway.

"You funny boy, how you don't know nobody down here. If you didn't, you wouldn't have been up here and the first place." She said smacking her lips.

"See that what's wrong with most of the world, we hear what we want, not what's said. I said I don't no nobody that live down here! And I don't, the reason I was down here was business." He said. Naomi just smiled on the other end of the phone. She loved a man who was slick with words.

"Ok boy you got me with that," she said letting him have it. "So, you gone come see me?" June asked.

"Come see you where?" She asked. If he didn't know anyone, then where was he staying? She prayed it wasn't where she thought.

"My hotel roo-" he started to say before she cut him off. "Not gone happen, you can come see me at my place that way I can control the environment." She said. June hit the blunt, and giggled at her, she was on point. He believed he'd have to work hard to get that pussy. But that was ok he loved a challenge. "Ok I'm cool with that, I'm in town is it cool if I fall through right now? " he asked. She looked at the clock it was Early but a part of her wanted to see him, so she threw caution to the wind and said it was ok. She said she would text the address.

June hung up and reclined back in his seat a little bit. As he drove through the town, he saw a few would be hood nigga in a few nice cars, and knew it was some money to be made down here. His phone ring and it was Kutta.

"What good skud?" He answered.

"Just wanna put you on point, it a lot going on in Chiraq right now bro. Nigga down here hurt over the dude Cash, and yo name all over that move. They saying you did him and his mom.....Man skud, Ion know what to say the guy's having a meeting tonight, to see what to do with you. Bro they try'na get you out the way my nigga. Lay low, I'm gone let you know more after tonight." Kutta said all in one breathe. He feared for June. This was something like never before, and the whole nation would be looking for revenge. "Damn skud I ain't have shit to do with that bro," June said.

"You know I know.... Just say low for me bro shit bout to get hot as hell." Kutta added.

"Ya I got you, I'm gone be in Ohio, get at me when you get a chance." June lied. He didn't want a soul knowing his whereabouts now with the nation looking for him the price tag on his head would be in the millions.

"That's a good look, do that. Love bro!" Kutta said.

"Love" June responded and disconnected the line. *What the fuck man,* he thought. Just when it was starting to look like shit was looking up for him, he was hit with another problem. He got a text alert on his phone; it was Naomi's address. June pushed his misfortunes to the back of his mind and placed his pistol on his lap. He still had business to attend to and wouldn't be scared outta get money. It was perhaps his only way outta his situation. He pulled up to her apartment on the west side of Madison and stepped out pistol in his hoodie pocket, with his hand squeezing it tightly. Before he knocked on the door Naomi opened it, looking marvelous. She'd taken the time out to really get herself together while awaiting his arrival. She wanted to make an impression and was successful from the expression on his face. "Come in," she said stepping aside. June walked in her home and notice it was well kelp. It smelled nice and he thanked god she was a clean woman. "I see you got all dolled up for me." She smirked. Naomi didn't respond just smiled and walked to the living room. "I ain't gotta worry bout know nigga popping up on me, do I? June asked, only half joking. "Boy you forcing it. This ain't that type of party. I ain't gotta set a nigga up, I got my own" she said in a matter a fact tone. June shock his head but still made note to check each room before he got too comfortable. When he came back Naomi rolled her eyes. "I hope I ain't offend you, it just a safety thing nothing person." He said taking a seat next to her. The second his ass hit the couch she was up on her feet. "Can I get you anything to drink?" She asked.

"Nah I'm good," he responded. Naomi took this opportunity to sit on the sofa across from him. " damn it's like that!" He asked.

"Kinda, I just don't wanna get to close. You only came over to get to know me not try'na fuck right?" She asked eyebrows raised.

"I'm a man of my word I came to get to know you nothing less nothing more." He said out his mouth, but his thoughts were different. *This gone be much longer then with Kim.*

* * * * *

It had been a long night of nonstop traffic, and the parking lot on Allied Dr. The night was spent with Marvell running in and out the house to meet Mike and his friends. Last night he made more than 2 thousand dollars and also found 5 more customs for his line. Marvell sat in his bed watching Paid and Full feeling like Ace Boogie. The story of rags to riches motivated him to stay up while the money rolled in. He looked at his product that was almost gone and called TT.

"What's good Tee?" TT asked as he answer the phone.

"We gotta link! I'm try'na get some move!" Marvell said, his eyes heavy. The only thing keeping him up was greed. "Where you at Tee," TT asked, getting up and going in the kitchen, and looking in the cabinet where he had a half brick.

"At my mom crib!" Marvell said, rubbing his eyes.

"I'm gone slide over there we need to talk anyways." TT said going to wash his face.

"Say no mo tee," Marvell said hanging up the phone and laying back on his bed. He closed his eyes for what only felt like a second, before his mom knocked on his door.

"What!" He yelled.

"TT here for you!" She said. Marvell looked at the clock and an hour had passed.

"Damn " he said getting up and going in the front room. TT stood their cup in hand while wearing a Blue, Green, and Pink Chanel vest, light blue jeans with holes and the knees, his shoes matched his vest. He also had a black man bag striped across his chest. Marvell like his style, well everything but the drug use.

"What you try'na spend?" TT asked, Looking over at Marvell mother. Marvell turned to see her standing there, "mom go in the back while I talk to tee," he said with more respect than she was used to. When she walked outta the room, TT pulled the brick out the bag taking a seat at the kitchen table. Marvell followed, before saying, "TT I don't know much about this shit I was hoping you'd put me up on game."

TT looked over at his lil homie, greed came to mind, but he decided to give Marvell the real.

"Look Tee, I get a hundred a gram from hypes when I sold bags. I'm gone sell you every oz for a thousand. You can make 2800 off each one." TT said. Marvell thought about it, he had more than 10 thousand dollars. If he spent that he'd have about 7 hundred dollars to his name, *Fuck it he thought he was going all in,* he thought.

"Give me 10 of em," he said. TT shook he head smiling at him. Marvell looked at him before saying, "what Tee? "

"I thought you was a lost cases Tee, all these years I been right here, and you never seem like you was gone get to it." TT said.

"I know I been watching you and waiting for my turn," Marvell said. TT looked at him proud he through the half brick on the table. "That 16 of em get me the other 6 bands when you get it." TT said, trying to help him get right. Marvell grabbed it and looked it over. It was a lot of work, but he was motivated more than ever." Say know mo tee good looking. " he said as TT took a sip of this drink and sat back. Marvell opened the bag and grabbed a piece of the coke to give his mother. He knew it was wrong but if she didn't get it from him, she'd get it somewhere else. Not that he was having it his self she would never have to bag for drugs again. When he walked in the room she was in bed.

"Hear you go ma," he said handing her and ball. She got up and grabbed it. Looking at him with questioning eyes.

"What this for?" She asked, not used to his behavior.

"It's for you, but take yo time with it ma, cause it all I got for you for now!" He said giving her a hug. He wanted to turn their relationship around, after leaving her behind after the shooting. His sister ready made him feel horrified with the notion of what could have happened to her.

"I love you ma," he said, walking out the room, leaving her stunned. When he came back in the kitchen TT was laid out on the couch easily in the morning. Marvell hated the effect the drugs had on his big homie.

* * * * *

Bee was awakened outta her sleep with a light knock on the door. She looked at the clock it was 11am. *Damn they get up early here* she thought going to the door in only her underwear. She opened it and closed it at the sight of her father. Danjunema close his eyes at the sight of his only in her underpants. "Come down stair when you're dress. We have business to attend to." Bee heard him say as she sat with her back against the door. "Okay be down soon." She yelled and went to get dress. 15 minutes later she was downstairs, and ready to learn her first lesson. When she entered the dining room, she spotted her new family at the table having brunch. Her mom looked stunning in a red Dior dress that was to die for. Her father was dressed in a black suit that was tailored to fit him perfectly. "have a sat baby," kia said warmly hoping to start building a motherly relationship with her child. Bee cast around a moment before taking a seat. Danjunema saw the express of disappointment on her face and decided to ease her worry's. "We will take care of business in a moment, but first we must take care of our bodies... So, take a second to feed your body, and it'll make it easier to focus throughout the day, while I feed your mind." Bee looked up at him, and smiled wondering what his excuse, would be for breaking his word. If Martez was still alive, she was leaving and never looking back. She couldn't stand to be lied to. Shit, they didn't even have enough space in her heart, to be forgiven for even the small mistakes. Bee sat there, and one of the many maids brought her a plate. She just looked at it, unable to eat at the moment. Bee was furious he could sit and eat like he didn't make a promise to her last night. *Who the fuck do they take me for? They must think I'm some young dumb bitch they can tell anything to*, she thought. Bee tried claiming herself down. She needed to relax and just see how things played out. Kia stood up and walked over to her. "I see you're not hungry? " she asked, concerned. Bee kept her head down looking at her plate. "Not really" she said. Danjunema stood up, "get the car ready." He yelled to one of his warriors." As he exited the room. "Try eating something before going with your father... You won't have much of an appetite afterwards." Kia said rubbing her back. This got Bee full attention, she looked at her mother," I've been able to eat right after murder. I'm sure I'll be able to eat after business." Bee said. Kia noticed the look in her eyes, she was a stone-cold killer, and nothing would affect her. Kia heart was broken, she'd allowed this to happen, the day she discarded her. She ran her finger though Bee's hair. "I understand but you might want to prepare yourself for this business baby, cause your father does it like no other." Kia said just as Danjunema walked in the room with his jacket on, followed by a gang of contract killer. "Are you ready baby girl?" He asked taking a deep breath. Bee looked at her mother one last time before standing to her feet. "Ya I am." She responded and followed him out the house. Bee couldn't forget those word Kia said, *your father does it like no other*, as she got and the back seat of the roll's royals. When she sat in it the seats seem to consume her body with softness. She watched as her father's soldiers piled into mini vans before he got in after her. He took the time to poor himself a drink before speaking. "Do you have the heart to do anything it takes to win?"

Bee thought about the question a split second before saying, "yes I do. I'm willing to do anything to get to the top." Danjunema glance over at her and smiled. "We will see!!!!!!! But I've got a surprise for you," he said as the motorcade pulled off. Bee was beginning to wonder if the surprise was what she thought. What if he really came through? Maybe he wasn't just an old Matherfucker running his mouth.

* * * * * *

"Yo ass is crazy!" Naomi said to June as he kelp up the pressure. He'd been shooting his shot hard. June pulled out his cellphone and began to watch a video on it. Naomi sat quiet for a while curious of what he was up to. "What so important in yo phone." She asked noisy. June understood this was his last chance to move things in the right direction. So, he didn't respond. "You heard me?" She asked.

"You say something?" He asked, using an old trick he'd been taught.

"What you watching?"

"Oh, just this video my friend sent me." He said going back to watching it. Naomi got up, wanting to see what had his attention. When she sat next to him, he was watching a porn movie. "On my god boy you nasty." She said but continued to watch. The girl on the video was being fucked from the back nice and hard. It was at this moment June turned the volume up and the sounds of sex fill the room. The woman was screaming in passion. "Damn he got a big dick." Naomi let slip about the 9-inch cock on the screen. June let her watch the video a while longer and placed his hand on her lap. When she didn't protest, he believed the porn was doing the job of turning her on. Her breathing began to stall, and he noticed lust in her eyes. "That ain't nothing," he said nonchalantly. Naomi looked away from the porn and stared him and the eyes. "That bigger than most." She said challenging him.

"Bigger than most, but not me." He responded without breaking eye contact.

"Prove it." She said. He sat the phone down and unbuttoned his jeans before pulling his 12-inch cock through his boxer briefs. Naomi sat there, mouth open. June took her hand and placed it on his dick. He held her wrist and moved her hand up and down. Naomi was so turn on, by the hard tool in her hand. She wanted to fight the fire burning deep within. But she'd reach the point of no return. June let go of her wrist, but she kept rubbing his cock. "Oh my god it so hard," she said. June let her stock him longer before asking her to take off her clothes. Naomi stood to her feet and slowly undress, as she glanced down on him. She stopped once she was nude and walked back to her bedroom. June took this as a sign to follow her and he walked into the room. He took the rest of his clothing off, before having her turn around so he could see her fat ass, he got behind her smacking her on the ass.

Smack!

"Oh, shiiit that feel good." She moaned.

Smack! Smack!

June swatted her ass really hard. She let out a cold cry. Naomi reached back hand grabbed a hold of his dick try'na place him inside her, but June knocked her hand away. And smacked it against her ass. "We ain't in a rush..... I'm gone take my time with you." He said. He licked his thumb and played with her asshole. *Ya here we go again* he thought about to fuck the shit outta her.

Chapter Six

* * * * *

B ee smile at the sight of Martez's head on the table inside the warehouse. She walked up to get a closer look. "I thought you was just bull shiting," she said more to herself then to him. "I don't bullshit. A man takes care of business and do anything to keep his word." He said standing exit to her. Bee bent down to look into Martez once handsome face it was mangled but she could still recognize the first man she'd ever loved. She made a promise to herself to never give her heart to another man. Heartbreak was the closest feeling to death she'd ever come. When she was hurting, she even thought about ending it all. But somehow, she pulled through and would never go through that again. "I don't want this life for you," Danjunema said. "I want you to be different from me and your mom, but I understand we are in no position to tell you how to live now. But I'll give you anything you want to step away from this lifestyle-" he added before being cut off.

"This is what I want.... I love this type of shit," she said poking Martez head with her fingers. Danjunema believed it was too late to change her now. He didn't want this, but he'd teach her the ropes. He waved his hard for one of his henchmen to take way the head, Bee's idolizing it was starting to make him uncomfortable. She looked up at him disappointed when it was taken, it reminded him of a child who'd lost their favorite toy.

"We have other business to attend to!" He said walking to a room in the back of the warehouse. Bee followed behind him in a room full of bricks of heroin. She peeked around amazed, her father was a boss, he'd proved that with the head alone. But this really sealed the deal, and her mind. She laughed inside at herself for doubting him. She Wonder how he sold all this and decided to ask.

"How do you move all this?" She asked taking a step forward and grabbing one of the bricks examining it. Danjunema walked up next to her and placed his hand on her shoulders. "I don't do shit but get it here, and let my team do the rest. Well, that's how it works now, that I have made a reputation for myself. I don't have to worry about someone stealing from me cause they know if they're caught...I'll murder their whole family. But back in the day I use to just sell it out of my store to loyal customers. It took years to build the operations you see today. You see I've stayed outta prison with treating this like a business. I plan my mission and think before I move. I ponder long and hard at night to determine new ways to say ahead of the police. I know they're constantly evolving, and I need to as well. You have to put the hours in to stay ahead. Just think of it like this there's somebody getting paid to spend a less 40 hour a week try'na lock kingpins up. So, it's up to us to put that much time or more planning." He said give just a little of the game. Bee thought about it, he was correct, she'd spent her short time and the games making short-term goals. Never once thinking about what would happen if she was locked up. She still had a lot to learn, and now that her father proved he was a man of his world, she'd give him the respect a man of his caliber deserve. "I never took the time think that far ahead" she said putting the brick back. "It's ok you're young and have time to learn. I'm gone to mentor you from this moment on and you'll run the family business when your Mother and I'm gone. " he said. Bee smiled this was unbelievable. Before going into the coma, she had no one, and wake up to a family. "I know we wasn't there for your childhood, but now we'll do better and anything you desire is yours until the day I die..." Danjunema said getting emotional, he cast into his child's eyes proud of how beautiful she'd turned out. But her heart scarred him. She appeared infatuated with murder, and it frighten him. Danjunema viewed slaughtering as part of doing business. Bee seemed to admire murder more than anything else. She had all the sign of masked murder who'd kill just for pleasure. He planned to show her the ropes and contain her love of blood.

"It's okay you're here now," she said giving him a hug. "I'm happy to have you guys in my life. I needed y'all. I spent years angry and alone, but none of that matters anymore. Y'all came back when I need y'all most! The future is all that matters daddy." She said letting go of him. When she pulled away a single tear run down his face. Danjunema rushed to wipe it away, it has been years since he shed a tear. But having his daughter in his life made him complete. "Thank you so much for giving us a chance... " he said. Bee held his face and her hands, "don't cry, its ok...." She said. Danjunema smiled at her before saying, "okay baby girl.... How bout you let me spend some quality time with my family. I know you're really looking forward to our lessons, but I just want to hang with you and your mother. " he said.

"That fine with me what you got in mine?" She asked.

"Your mom loves shopping. And I feel I have years of gifts to make up." He said.

"I can shop," she warned him.

"I got enough money to last a few generations." He said, because money wasn't in issue.

"Then let shop," Bee said.

* * * * *

June sat back on Naomi's couch in his boxers. She was in the kitchen making him something to eat. He'd spent over an hour dicking her down. Naomi came out the kitchen wearing nothing but a thong. June licked his lips at her, the pussy was good as hell. She smiled at him and gave him the plate.

"Thanks" he said taking a bite outta the chicken. *Damn the bitch can cook to,* he thought.

"Nah, thank you," she said, sitting next to him." I didn't know how much I needed that. It's been too long. Seeing that porn made me so damn hot, I couldn't help myself..." She paused, "I hope this don't make you think I'mma hoe?" She said, a little ashamed of what took place. June sat the chicken down and licked his fingers. "Nah, I don't think that I could tell you wasn't from how tight that pussy was." He lied. Her shit was tight but that didn't mine anything, these females wasn't slow, they know how to make that pussy bounce back. Naomi was delighted to hear that, in the way he said it turned her on.

"I'm gone take a shower," she said getting up headed for the bathroom. "Wait come here, I gotta ask you something. She turned around and June pulled her on his lap. "It's hustlers up here?" He asked.

"Ya, nigga's come up here from Chicago all the time. Its people from all around down here try'na get some money." She said.

"Where they be at?" He asked.

"I don't know much but my brother does. You can meet him if you want, I could introduce y'all." She said putting her arms around his neck.

"What he be on?" He questioned, hoping he was getting some money. If that was the case, he was hoping to become his new plug.

"He just be with his friends."

"Oh, that's what's up," June said pretending to give a fuck.

"I know!" She said getting up "is that all," she asked with her hands on her hips, "cause a bitch gotta clean her pussy. " she added.

"Ya my bad ma," June laughed.

"Is you gone be here when I get out?" She asked.

"That's up to you, do you want me to be?"

"Ya I want you to be." She said.

"Then I'll be here" he said. Naomi spun around and went to the bathroom. June lit up a blunt, his mind went to all the challenges he had. He was faced with His biggest challenge ever. He was scared, cause he couldn't war with the whole mob. So he needed to stay alert and stay as low as possible. That was the best solution to this war to get money and keep his head low. He thought about how Chicago would never be safe for him again. How he could be in outcast against his own. He could only imagine the stories, that would be spoking of him. They would portray Cash as a fallen king and a good leader, and him as a trader. People who once admired him, would now cast stone. It was crazy how just a week ago he was next up, and now he was and outcast. He was hurt by the turn of events but would live with them. June turned on the TV and laid his head back watching the news. It was the same shit going on in the world people getting killed and people going to jail. The President was still offending everyone. He closed his eyes to rest them awhile....... *Cash walked into the building holding a bag of money and handed it to June." How much is this bro?" June asked walking down the hallway to their trap." Ion know, that's what we gone find out in a minute." Cash said, he'd just rob a plug and Wisconsin and shot straight down to Chicago. June opened the door and inside the house was a group of teens smoking weed. Cash followed him to the back room and took a seat on the twin-size mattress. June opened the bags and took out a stack of bills and handed it to cash before taking one for his self. They began counting the money and silence. "A bro.." Cash said. June looked up mad he fucked up his count. "when I come up, I'm gone take you with me." Cash added. June looked at his big homie and laughed." Here you go with this other shit, I know we gone hit the top together. But we ain't gone get there if we spend more time talking then counting cash!" June jocked.* "June" Naomi's yelling brought him to the present. "what good" he said. Naomi jumped back and he realized he was pointing his pistol at her. "Damn my bad," he said. What the fuck did she get herself involved in; Naomi wondered. June put the gun on his waistband and got up. He pulled her close while she continued to look stunned. "My bad ma," he said once their chest was pressed together. " I want to share something with you..." He said pausing for a second and starred in her eyes." I been through a lot to be so young. I gotta be on point, so I keep this on me. He added patting his waistband. "I know what I'm doing with it so if somebody get shot it want be a mistake." He said try'na easy her fears. She just looked at him, unable to find words. She'd saw a gun before but never had one pointed her way.

June placed a soft kiss on her lip unsure of what else to do or say. He didn't want this situation to run her off. She was a mayor part of his new plan." We good ma?" He asked kissing her again. She pulled back and looked into his eyes. "Ya, just don't do that again." She said.

"You got that" he said kissing her once more.

"I'm gone get me a room to stay at while I'm down here," he said switching the subject. Naomi glanced into his eyes with sadness. She didn't want to see him go, but he couldn't live with her. Her brother wasn't having it. Even though she was a grown woman, he was overprotective of her. "Can you say just a little longer." She asked.

"Nah I can't, but if you want you can come show me around the city, and maybe if you're good you can spend the night out with me." He said jockey. She smiled, "then I gotta be good," she said licking her lips seductively. "I hope so," he said smacking her ass check and hold them tight pulling her close." Go get dress so we can head out," he added taking a seat on the couch.

Naomi took 15 minutes to get dressed; when she walked out the room with her long hair and a bun and some leggings that fit her body perfectly. June smile and stood up," ya I see you try'na spend the night," he said starring her down. Naomi noticed the lust in his eyes, he looked like he wants to attack her and rip off her clothing to fuck right on the spot. She treasured the effect she possesses over man, and even though she wanted to fuck him again, it would have to wait." I'm just being a good girl, " she mocked, grabbing her car keys." Nah you riding with me," June said giving her his car keys. He didn't like the concept of people pulling up on them because they recognized her car. He wanted to move around unnoticed.

"Ok so where we headed," she asked opening the door. June followed her outside and watched as she locked up. "You gone show me around my new kingdom." He said excited to begin his take over.

* * * * *

Marvell was in the house while his phone rang nonstop. It was crazy how he'd been running his self-thin since he started trapping, he barely got sleep. Every time he closed his eyes a call came in, and he was too hungry to let any amount go uncollected. If it was $10 or more, he was getting it no questions asked.

He done the math on the coke and planned on spending 5 thousand to get his first car as soon as he made it. He picked up the stack and counted it again. He only needed $50 more dollars and the car would be his. Once he was able to move freely, he'd pay TT, before saving the rest. Marvell went on Facebook to return a message from a female he'd been messaging the last few days. As soon as he got his new whip, he was gone scoop her up. He was thankful his mom agreed to put the car in her name for him. He been showing more respect to her hoping to heal their unhealthy relationship. It had been a while since their father was murder over her drug debt, and it was time he forgave her. She was sick and couldn't help herself. He would keep what she needed that way he didn't have to be out there stealing and tricking. She didn't know he was aware that she'd allow people to use her body for dope. They never spoken of it but the whole family was aware of what too place them late nights she'd spend walking up Allied with no money, only to be seen getting in a car with a stranger and coming home with drugs and money. It used to kill his sister she'd spend the night crying her heart out. Marvell would hold her and say things would get better. But she was old enough to know better. His sister knew the odds of a drug addict getting clean wasn't good. They only got clean two ways once they were dead or in jail. Marvell always had his mother back, but the loss of his father changed their relationship dramatically. It was at this point that he started to disrespect her and curse her out. Things he was starting to regret. Marvell believed a strong person treated other with respect, and he wanted to be that person. It was time to change from a boy into a man and take care of his family.

Marvell phone ring, it was a customer he'd nicknamed blue face, cause he never spent less than a hundred.

"What's good?" He asked.

"The usual." Blue face said.

"Pull through," he said, hanging up. Blue face had called a few times today and knew he had to come to Allied. Marvell smiled happy to have enough to get his car. He'd spotted a black 06 two door Monte Carlo (MC) with low miles he had plans to sit it up and put rims on it. It was also dear cause the nickname was his gang. He went to his mother's room she was in bed, sleeping. Marvell took a seat next to her and kissed her cheek waking her up.

"Ma, I need you to go with me to get his car!" He said. He was gone give blue face a few free bags to give him a ride to the car lot.

"Ok baby give me a second to get up!" She said glad to be able to do something for her son.

"Ok ma," he said, going back to his room excited to get his first car at 15 years old.

The game turned things around quick and it was only the beginning. With time there was no telling what the future held.

Chapter Seven

* * * * *

(Chicago)

It was a rainy day and to the true believer's god was morning the loss of a great man. The sky seemed to represent the pain of Chicago. Slim walked into the funeral home, and it was packed from wall to wall, and there was a group of people outside in the rain to show their respect. Slim took his seat in the front row. He viewed at the castes of a falling king. He thought about how cash believed in his dream before anyone else, Cash invested in Bagz Of Money, when they had nothing, and helped it become what it was today. They still had a long way to go before they were a household name; he wouldn't give up until it was done. He owe that much to Cash. His goals would remain the same and that was to get their first big hit and the music business. The pastor strolled in the room like he was the creator born again, and everyone fell silent the instant he approached the podium. He picks up the Bible and waved it and the air, showing the crowd, or sinners.

"The LOUD, give and he take. We don't know why he call some of us home earlier than others." He began putting the Bible down. And walking from behind the podium. "But he called a great young man to join his side. I see the heartache in this room. He was loved, I see it in the tears being shed. That pain will fade in time."

Was the last thing slim heard the pastor say for drifting off into his own thoughts. He looked around the room some people were pouring their hearts out, and others appeared ready to slide the second the funeral was over. The tone in the room was like the world was ending, people seemed defeated. For over an hour family members and friends got up and told stories of the impact he had on them. By the end slim had shed a few tears as well. He got up went out back to join the motorcade or vehicle about to take cash on his last ride through Chicago. There were over a hundred luxury automobile line up in front of the Hurst waiting for Cash body to be placed inside. Slim got inside his ATS 500 Gt and played R-Kelly "I wish" low.

He peeked at all the car and thought about how Cash would love the turn out. He would be amazed at how much love he was receiving. Slim grabbed his blunt and lean back in his seat. Today they would morn tomorrow they'd meet, AND THE FOLLOWING DAY THEY'D WAR. Cash's murder had to be avenged for the BD's to save face. The orders would come from the top.

A horn honked getting his attention, he lifted up in saw Cash's remains being placed in the hurst. Someone honked their horn of their car 3 times and the remaining cars followed honking theirs 6 times one after another. When they made it to Slim, he followed showing his respect.

Slowly the cars pulled off one at a time, and drove through the streets, they made their way through every one of their hoods and every time they bent a block a crowd awaited them. People were throwing up the tre's, as if they was saluting a falling soldier. "Rest in Peace King Cash" was being chanted. Slim noticed how Cash was loved and smiled. It was a sight to see. They went through the south side of Chicago before stopping on 35th & state where Cash had been raised. The buildings where long gone, but the land still had value to the people raise here. After about 2 minutes they pulled off heading to burry a king.

Meanwhile

June laid back as Naomi drove, he was smoking a blunt and starring out the window. The city was too small to have all the shit transpiring Naomi spoke about. She told him about a block that was moving bricks named Allied. When they pulled through it 15 minutes ago, he didn't believe it, cause it was empty. But Naomi pulled into a parking lot and pointed out all the traffic going into one building. It didn't take long for him to recognize the game when we saw it. Naomi said it's like that 24\7 *I'm gone do my thing out here* he thought as they continued to drive around the town. One thing he loved was the police didn't seem like they was racially profiling like in most small cities. He glanced over at Naomi she was so sexy. He wonders why she was single. But brushed the thought to the back of his mind.

Ring!

June looked down at his line and saw Kutta number, so he quickly answered. "What good skud? He asked how the funeral was.

"Shit all bad down here skud, no lie this shit outta hand to keep it real. The whole city came out for this nigga funeral. We in some shit bro cause they on yo ass down here. All type of nigga came up to me talking like then gone slid when they see you. I let that shit go at the moment, but kelp the names and my mind. We gone do the sliding on them before they can even think about bring harm yo way. So, don't worry about that. Just hold yo head and say low until we able to make it back up there." Kutta said sincerely. He fought hard not to speak his mind when nigga's was talking bout what they were gone do to his brother. That shit had him so angry they plan to start sliding on people tonight. He just couldn't wait to put somebody down.

"Ya nigga's got ball's now??? " June said ready to get back to the city and remind them how he gets down. They must've forgot he dropped nigga's for entertainment. Kutta heard the anger in his voice and smiled. He admitted June was something else even when the whole mob was against him, he wasn't scared, always ready to put his murder game down. A lot of people would just run but June was ready to wage war with whoever.

"Nah they just pretending bro! But we gone fix that so don't worry bout it skud." Kutta said hoping to calm June down. "Everybody that said something slick I'm gone get on ASAP, that's on Dave. You just keep getting that money" Kutta added.

"Man, that shit got me pissed bro, I ain't have shit to do with it either." June said pulling his pistol from his pocket and placing it on his lap.

"I know skud" Kutta said. June other line start to blink, he looked at it and saw Black's number." A bro I'm gone hit you back," June said, before clicking over.

"hello," he said. "Where you at?" Black asked. She woke up and he was gone, and she wanted to make sure he was ok.

"In Madison." He said.

"Oh ya? Why you ain't take me?" She asked.

"I ain't know you wanted to come." He answered.

"Why wouldn't I want to boy? Let me find out you forgot I'm from down there." She said playfully. June laughed inside cause he had forgotten, "damn ma I did! No lie." He said. When he glanced over, he saw Naomi shaking her head an rolling her eyes. But paid it no attention, "I'm gone come get you tomorrow, cause I'm gone be down here for a while." He said.

"Okay you do that cause it's lame as hell up here by myself," Black confessed.

"You know I got you!" He said before getting off the phone with Black. Naomi was all in this mouth, but he wasn't gone explain shit to her. She seemed to leave it alone or so he thought but then they pulled up to her house and she jumped out and rushed inside furious. "That's why that bitch single he said to his self before getting in the driver seat and pulling off. If she thought, he was gone kiss her ass she had another thing coming. To be honest, he didn't need her since Black was from Madison. Black could show him around. "Ya fuck that bitch" he said, and decided to go get Black right now, at less he could trust her.

Later that night Chicago

Kutta lay in the brushes while Bullet sat in the getaway car a block away. He'd sent over an hour their waiting for his victim to come out the house. When the door opened it wasn't who he expected, *damn* he thought. The young lady made it down the stairs but before the door close his victim followed behind her. Kutta delayed until they exited the gate around the house, and was on the sidewalk, before jumping out the cut mask on, pistol in the air and murder on his mind. The look in the man's eyes when he stared down the burrow of the pistol was priceless. After all the shit he was talking earlier, he was frozen now. But the woman wasn't, she reached and pulled a pistol out her jacket pocket. Kutta reaction was swift, he turned and double tapped hitting her twice in the chest. Her body dropped quicker, than a ton of bricks. When he turned, dude was already halfway up the block. Kutta didn't give chase, he just stood over her in shot her once more, before running back to the car in Bullet pulled off.

"Man, I ain't even get him." Kutta said disappointed.

"What?"

"A bitch upped, and I put her down, but that's gave the nigga time to get away."

Bullet started laughing, " she was a ride or die for real" he joked.

"I know right! Gotta get one like that" Kutta said laughing as well.

"What next?" Bullet asked.

"We keep on sliding, " Kutta answered.

"I knew you was gone say that, that's why I came up over here." Put yo mask back on here go that nigga Tom Tom, one the corner." Bullet said. Kutta saw him and rushed to throw his mask on. Tom Tom saw the masked man jump out the car and took off running, but Kutta was determine not to let another one get away. He stopped and aimed.

Boom! Boom!

When he saw feathers fly out his jacket he believed he'd hit him. But Tom Tom kept running a few more steps before falling to the ground. Kutta ran over to kill him when he heard police sirens and saw flashing lights coming down the block. His heart dropped but he was gone do what he came to. He shot Tom Tom two more time and the back of the head, before aiming at the police.

Boom! Boom! boom!

Kutta took off running to the getaway car, as the police officer got out and aimed at him. Bullet jumped out the car and fired at the cop making him duck behind his crosier, giving Kutta enough time to make it to the car. Bullet jumped inside and pulled off as Kutta continued to fire shots at the cop until they were able to turn the Corner. The cop tried giving chase but the rounds to the vehicle blew the engine. He slammed his fist against the horn, "damn," he yelled.

"Is he behind us?" Kutta asked his heart jumping outta his chest. "Hell, naw" Bullet said hitting corner after corner, try'na get to his brother house. "We gotta hide this whip, call my brother and tell him we pulling up hot, and need to get in the garage." Kutta called and told him they were less than a block away, and to let them in before hanging up. When they pulled up a few seconds later Bullet brother was alert, and they parked the car outta sight before rushing inside the house.

"Man, what the fuck y'all just do?" Cortez asked, the second the door slammed behind everyone. Cortez was a lame, and Bullet wouldn't have got him involve in this if he didn't have to.

"Man, the less you know the better bro!" He said and took a seat. Kutta followed when he looked up at Cortez he was understandably pissed off. But he ain't say nothing and walked to the back of the house shaking his head. Bullet kelp his head down until they were alone.

"How mad he looked? " he asked Kutta.

"He was pissed." Kutta said wiping some of the sweat from his forehead on his shirt.

"Damn bro ain't gone fuck with me after this one." Bullet said. He understood how things appeared in his brother's eyes. The only time he came around he was in some bullshit.

"Man bro love you, my nigga, ya'll gone be good just give him time to cool off." Kutta said before giggling.

"What's funny" Bullet wondered.

"No bullshit, bro got outside fast as hell. " he laughed, and Bullet couldn't help but laugh." No bullshit, that's how I know bro love you. He thought you was in trouble and didn't think twice about coming to your add." Kutta added.

* * * * *

June arrived in Beloit a few hours ago, he was in the bed with Black just laying back smoking a blunt and talking. They decided not to go back to Madison until tomorrow. Black was filling him in on more painful time and her life, they even talked about Cash for the first time. Black saw his funeral happened today while she was on Facebook. R.I.P statuses where all over her timeline. She was a little mad at June for not informing her they was laying him to rest today, but she didn't complain. She noticed the stress on June face and didn't want to add to it. June eyes watered while talking about Cash, Black felt his pain. When she had enough of telling sad story from long ago, she asked, "so Cash brought you up like family? If so, how things get so fucked up between y'all?"

June passed her the smoke and set up. "Bro just changed. He got to looking down on us when he started getting money and was holding us back at one point. But then it all changed after his bother got killed. It seems like he changed for the better. Then he got shot and switched up again. We were good until we got into it right before he passed." June said reflecting on their history. Black rubbed his back, "June it's ok to miss him," she said.

"Nah fuck that nigga," June said on an emotional roller coaster. He did miss Cash and was hurt about the loss, but Cash put a hit on him before he died, and he'd never get pass that. Black walked over to him pulling him into her arms. June held her tight, lost in his emotions. He'd lost the closest thing to a father he'd ever known now and couldn't grave because of how crazy their relationship had become. He was confused cause there was hate in his heart, but good memories in his mind. They were having tough times, but the times didn't always use to be that way. A tear fell from his eyes, as he began to break down expressing his true emotions. Black saw the tear and couldn't stop her tears from pouring out. She'd never saw a man cry before, and him being vulnerable in front of her made her see him in a new light. "Let it out," she said. It was at that moment she'd began to shed tears for Glory. Then she realized she was holding her killer. Black released him and set back on the bed. June looked at her and noticed her tears for the first time.

"Why you have to kill her," she asked, unable to look at him. June wiped the tear from his eyes. He believed this conversation would come up one day and still wasn't prepared for it. Black looked at him with a sadness. "She was a really good person." She added.

June looked at her, "I can't tell you why, just know it's the only kill I regret... I see her face when I close my eyes at night... That kill cased me the love of my life... I'm sorry for taking her from you, even though I don't know her, I know you and your pain is enough to make me sorry." He said. Tears poured from her eyes. She didn't expect him to be sorry. This made it so hard to be mad at him even though she wanted. "I know we got off to a fucked-up start, but I hope we can move past it in become friends. One thing about me is I'm loyal to people I fuck with, and I ride for mine. If we start over, I'm gone need your forgiveness to forgive me for my fuck up." Black thought about it a second. Its didn't take long to make a decision; he was the only friend she had. " Its behind us she said standing up and embracing him. Black forced any thoughts of the past life out her mind. June was her family now. Black decided to change the subject, "so what's the plan for Madison?" She asked.

"You gone show me around while I take over." He replied glad to move away from the topic.

"If I'm gone help, I need in," she said seriously. June smiled, and shook his head okay. " how much we talking about?" He asked. Black thought for a moment, she wasn't try'na get paid for showing him the town. No, that was thinking small, and would be a onetime check. She wanted in on the entire thing. " I want to put up money to buy in," she said. June frowned his face up, confused. "I got the work I don't need yo money." He said, "all I need is you to show me around!" he added. Black wasn't about to take know for answers, so she pleaded her case. " I got, 300,000 " she said, "it all your if you put me in play. I wanna be able to buy some work and push it, with your help." She added.

"You got 300,0000 racks?" June questioned.

"Ya, " she said praying he'd give her a chance.

"I got you." He said, unable to turn down the cash. "But you gone have to buy your work from me and only me!" He added.

"That's fine!" She said, just happy being able to make her own living. Black believed her saving wouldn't last long with the way she spent it.

"This how it's gone work, I'm gone cut you in on 20% of what we come across together. The other 80% we sell my shit." He said.

"30%" Black said. June looked her up and down, before smiling. He liked her style, she spotted an opportunity and seized it.

"I can do that for you!" He said. Black stood up and put out her hand for him to shack. June took it and they concealed the dill. "now get some sleep we got a big day ahead of us." He said.

Chapter Eight

* * * * *

They woke up and headed out first thing in the morning. It was a cool morning with a light breezy. The sun was behind clouds, which gave the day more of a fall feeling, but it was mid-summer. On the ride to Madison June phone was blown up by Naomi. Damn *this bitch blowing me up* he thought, Black shook her head believing it was a woman call back-to-back. The dick was good, so chances were the woman was more addicted to that than him." Boy just answer it. She ain't gone stop calling until you do." Black said. June glanced over at her before looking back out the window. "Who said it was a bitch? " he said.

"Boy it a bitch, ain't know nigga calling you like that!" She said. June phone rang again. He picked it up this time, "fuck is you blowing my line up for shorty," he said upset.

"Where you been?" Naomi asked like she was his woman. June pulled the phone off his ear and stared at it. "I ain't gotta tell you shit," he said putting the line back to his ear. Black peeked over wondering what was being said on the other end of the phone. She felt anguish for whoever it was, because it was clear whatever they felt for him he didn't feel in return.

"So, you think you just gone fuck me and play me." Naomi yelled into the phone. June laughed, "ya that's the plan shorty," he said hanging up the phone. Not even a second later it was ringing again. "Looks like you gone need a new phone," Black jived. June just shook his head.

About an hour later they arrived downtown Madison at Black apartment. The high-rise building was one of the tallest in Madison. The capital was clearly visible from her apartment. It was months since she'd been home, and if she hadn't paid the rent a year in advice, she would've lost everything. "Damn you say downtown?" June asked. Black turned off the engine, before shaking her head yes. Then open the door and step out the car. June shadowed her as they entered the building and took the evaluator to her floor. The building was nice, but not like downtown Chicago, he thought. But it wouldn't be a bad headquarters for his operation. They entered her apartment, and it was pleasant enough. Black went to the back room and retrieve the duffle bag, she took 50,000 and place it under her bed, before taking June the rest.

"That's 300,000 right there." She said handing it to him. June took the bag and glanced inside. The money was nicely stacked with nothing but 100$ bills. " so, we good you gone plug me and make sure nothing happens to me?" She asked for confirmation.

"I got you, you good!" He said putting the bag over his shoulder.

"So, when I'm gone get the loud?" She asked. "loud?" He asked. "Black I ain't fucking with no weed, I'm pushing heroin and coke," he added. She understood what he meant but never sold it before. "I don't want that I'm looking for some good smoke." She said.

"I don't know if I could get any but let me make a few calls." He said picking up his phone to call Kia.

"Hello!" She said.

We need another meeting" he said.

"Already?" She asked.

"Ya but bout something else." He responded.

"Where and when?" She asked.

"Same place, Madison if you want."

"That's fine I'm on my way up there today anyways." She said, "I'll call you when I arrive." she added, before hanging up. Black gone to the kitchen while he was on the phone. When June strolled in, she was taking out a snack from the cabin. He told her to pass him one and she throw him a pack of grandma cooks. Before taking a seat at the table.

"So, is you gone be able to find what I'm searching for? "she asked.

"Ya I'm gone see in a while, but I don't see why not. What I'm gone do is use your money to get you the move, then I'm gone just take a 20% cut for making sure you safe," he said. Black smirked at the thought of getting 80% instead of 30%.

"Whenever you ready I can just introduce you to the nigga's up here getting money. I know everybody already. We just gone have to ride around and bump into them since I ain't got my old phone no more." She said.

"Say know mo I could do that. That's a lot easier than what I had in mind." He said. Black could only imagine what he had in mind. One thing she believed was it involved murder.

"Ya let's just do it my way we don't need the heat you gone bring." She said.

June took some of his cooks out the bag, without responding. Black walked to her room leaving him alone. She went to her closet and picked out a black jumpsuit, before changing into it. She marched over to the mirror and looked at herself. Thoughts of Bee came to mind. She reminisced on times they hustling dress like thugs. *Well sexy thugs* she thought.

She planned for things to be different this time, she wouldn't be the weak link this go around. She walked into the kitchen June was still seated at the table deep in thought. "I need a pistol!" She said breaking his thought process. June shook his head she reminded him of Kim, so much.

* * * * *

Marvell sat behind the wheel of his first car smiling hard as hell. You couldn't tell him he wasn't the flyest nigga in the world inside his 14-year-old vehicle. The black insides in red paint was clean, and even though he was only 1 year older than the whip it was his.

A green 2019 Maserati Levante Granlusso pulled and the lot and he saw TT behind the wheel smiling. Marvell got out to admire it, as TT stepped out as well.

"Damn TT, this you?" He asked.

"Since when you know me to drive something that ain't mine?" TT answered his question with a question.

"When you get this?" He asked opening the passenger door to get a look inside.

"About an hour ago! I heard you got something, so I wanted to do the same." TT said only telling the half of it. He'd head Marvell got a car and even though his old car a 2017 Chevrolet Camaro was a lot better, than Marvell new car, it wasn't new. He wanted to show Marvell up for some weird reason that even he couldn't explain. But what he didn't know was Marvell wasn't in competition with no one. He didn't even notice, what TT was up to. His mind was content with life and growing up with nothing he'd always been at the bottom. So, he didn't know how competitive the streets could get. TT looked at him and noticed the excitement in his eyes.

"Damn TT this bitch nice you gone fuck em up with this move." Marvell said happy for his big homie. TT began to feel lame for wanting to ruling Marvell's moment. He didn't know why he felt the need to shit on him at time. He wasn't used to Marvell having shit and some part of he was hating.

TT made a mental note to kill that shit before it got outta hand. A lot of friends fell out over competing with each other.

"Ya we gone get you one you keeping going hard " he said, to convince his self he was a good friend.

"I'm cool for now, I'll get one when it's my time," Marvell said, happy with his ride.

"You wanna take it for a ride." TT asked.

"I'm cool tee, I'm try'na get like you and never drive shit that ain't mine." Marvell added.

"I'm feeling that tee," TT said, while lining back on the car. Marvell phone ringed, "who?" He said knowing it was money." Cool, cool say know more I'm gone pull up on you in 10 minutes." He added hanging up the line. TT watched his every move; Marvell was moving like a new man.

"That bitch be knocking," TT said, as Marvell went in his pocket giving him 3 thousand, he made over night, "I'm have the rest soon!" He said getting in his car in pulling off. TT was left there feeling, uneasy about Marvell newfound hustle.

Meanwhile

Slim arrived at the meeting and what he saw was unbelievable. The number of people was in the thousands standing outside by their cars, and it was at this instant he noticed what the full forces of the nation looked like. He Parked and got out and walked towards the park. Where he was stopped by a few big guards. "Where you from?" One of them asked, "35th and state" slim said.

"What's yo name?" The other one questioned.

"Slim" the first one glanced in his phone for a minute before telling the other one he was good. Slim walked into the building and sat alone in the corner waiting for the assembly to get started. He pulled out a blunt and flamed it up. But a few seconds later someone approach him informing him, there wouldn't be any smoking. They wanted everyone to have a comprehendible mind. He did as he was told and relaxed in his set. Slim watch as the building slowly crowded. The room was set up like a graduation with chairs nicely lined up and rows. To the blind eye it looked like anything but what it truly was. When the room was stuff and everyone was in their set an older man in his late 60's stood on the stage, and the room went silent. The old man appeared more like a businessman than a thug. He was light skin with light drown eyes. His 5'10 frame was solid from workouts. He had confidence, and swagger of and old school player. There was a big picture of June across a screen on the side of the stage with the world greenlight on it.

"Take a good look at his face." The old man said pointing at the screen. "This is the trader who killed Cash for the people who don't know." He paused to let his word sink in." This the reason the opps laughing at us..... They saying there ain't loyalty amongst us. They even saying we done seen our last great leader. To that I laugh!!!!Cash was a great person, but he was only the face, that allowed us old heads to reach a younger generation. He wasn't our leader though! He play his roll and for that he'll always have my respect, and he should have yours as well. That's why we must act quickly in his memory." He said. Slim was stunned to hear these words coming from the old head. He wondered who he was, as if he was reading his mind, he said. "I know a lot of y'all don't know who I am and that how I prefer it. Don't nothing happen without me knowing about it." he said hitting his chest hard with his fist. "I step out the shadows to say things will be okay, we are stronger together. And anyone who plan on taking the side of this backstabber will be laid next to him when this is all said and done. Ain't none of us bigger than the mob and if you think you is, it won't be long until you family putting you in a box. To the once that's loyal to June, I want you to turn him over before you find yourself in over your head." He said as spit flu from his mouth. He spoke with so much passion Slim felt his words in his soul." I'm gone say one last thing before I get outta here. I don't want a bag sold until dude gone. Anybody sells a slug get a plunking head." He said, before strolling out the room followed by 50 other soldiers. When he was out the room it was filled with questions bout who he was. But no one seemed to really know the answer. Slim stood to his feet and exited the building. He was as confused as the rest of them but wasn't to invest, and the situation.

* * * * *

Kutta stood up after the old heads left the room and looked at bullet. Bullet just sat there discombobulated, and unable to stand to his feet. The news was unbelievable. Cash had been the boss, right? What the fuck was the old nigga talking about. What blew their minds was people they'd saw with Cash, was standing alone side the old head. Bullet stood to his feet," bro let's get the fuck outta here," he instructed Kutta in they headed for the exit. Once they were inside the car, they spoke for the first time." Bro what the fuck was that?" Bullet asking turning on the car and pulling off. Kutta didn't know what to say, he just sat there thinking the same thing." Bro we gotta call June and let him know what just happened." bullet added. Kutta took out his phone and called June.

"What to it skud?" June asked.

"You still in Madison?" Kutta asked.

"Ya."

"We on our way up there right now. Shit just got crazy at the meeting, we coming down for a while cause ain't shit moving down here until you out the way some old head said." Kutta slit out.

"What old head?" June asked.

"Don't know skud, that's the fucked-up part. Never seen him a day in my life." Kutta said rubbing his waves.

"Say know mo, make sure don't nobody following y'all before coming into town." June said being alert.

"You know that" Kutta said before hanging up the phone. Bullet looked over at him," damn skud, once we leave the city more than likely we gone have a greenlight on us too." Bullet said. Kutta stared him up and down. "what's you mean by that? " he asked questioning Bullet loyalty.

"Don't do that skud, I'm just making sure you know what the move is." Bullet said angry Kutta thought he had disloyalty in his heart. After all they'd been through, for him to second guess him was devastating. Bullet glanced over at Kutta with hate and disappointment in his eyes. Kutta felt him starring, "You got something to say say it bro," he said. Bullet didn't respond, because anything he said would end a friendship and didn't wanna speak while upset. They rode in silence to pick up the bricks from the trap, before jumping on the expressway.

* * * * *

The BP gas station wasn't one of the large company finest locations. It had seen better day. But it was the tipple hood convenience store run down, but always packed with customers. June and Black was there as, Black set outside the car talking to a tall ugly man wearing a few chain with VS stones. He was also riding in a Porsche. June watched her hand him a sample of the work he'd giving her to pass out. June was giving away coke to prove he had good product and wasn't the police. He knew hustlers wouldn't be quick to trust a new plug and town. So, this would move things alone quicker. Black came back to the automobile and hoped in and pulled away. "He say if its right he gone call." She said. June was feeling good, his work was proper so that wasn't a problem.

They spent the last few hours riding around and bumped into a few hustlers Black said was up. If they all called it was a possibility that he'd have a footing in the city. If not, they'd just keep at it.

June phone ring, he glanced down and noticed Kia number.

"I'm up here," she said once he answered.

"I'm gone get a room; I could use some dick after we take care of business." Kia said. June thought about how good her pussy was the first time and didn't have a problem with her request.

"Just let me know where to meet you and I'm game!" He said.

"I'm gone go to the hotel you was at the last time." She said.

"Cool when you want me there?"

"Bout 30 minutes!" She said.

"Cool." June said hanging up the phone. He looked at Black I'm gone need you to take me somewhere then slide back on me and a few hours. "June said.

"Okay, I'm gone do some shopping while I wait." She said, before adding, "where I'm taking you."

"Best Western on gammon rd." He said. Black hit a U-turn at the next light, heading to the westside.

Twenty minutes later they arrived at the hotel, and Black noticed a black Lamborghini. It was outta place and she believed whoever was driving it, June was there to meet. June opened the door got out before telling Black to stay close just in case he needed to leave sooner then he thought. She asked him if he wanted her to sit outside for a while, but he declined. June walked into the hotel and called Kia to see what room she was in. She told him 253 and he walked down the hall. The door was slightly a jar and he entered the room. What he saw was amazing, Kia was on the bed naked. It was a sight out this world, she turned around making her ass clap for him. The way it waved with every movement made him stand there with a hard cock and seconds. Kia glanced over her shoulders and said, "Come take care of this," before smacking her ass. June took his time walking over to her too slowly to demonstrate control, but his dick was fighting to break free from his pants. When he got over to the bed, he stood behind her as she kept tweaking. He snaked her ass hard and she jumped but didn't stop moving. "That felt good do it again." She said. June swatted it again as he began to undress. Kia turned around wanting to see his big tool up close. When he pulled it out she smiled, remembering what occurred last time. The way it invaded her inside and made her cum long and hard. She couldn't wait to fill it inside her walls again. June stocked his cock, loving the lust in her eyes. "You want it, don't you?" He asked. Kia reached out with both hands and rubbed the side with her nails. June treasured how it felt and removed his hand. Kia took control and looked up in his eyes. "I've wanted it since I left last time," she said. June stared down at the beautiful older woman, holding his dick in her hands, she was dangerous. She had blood on her hands and was a scored lover and killed one lover already that he knew of. But at that instant none of that mattered, while she stocked him. The only thing he wanted was for her to put him in her mouth. Kia played with him licking up and down his dick, making sure to use a lot of spit. She put the long thickness in her mouth, wanting to taste it.

"Stop playing shorty and suck it," he said.

"When I'm ready! I'm the one in control here..." She said. June liked how she put him and his place. He'd let her have her fun now in later he'd show who was in control. "You got that" he said. Kia jagged him with long slow stocks. "I want you to fuck me nice and hard for an hour. Then I wanna suck your dick for an hour." She said licking her lips. "I can do that. But after that we getting down to business." He added.

"All business and no play with something as fun as this!" She said giving him a big lick from ball to the head.. "Nah, we gone have a lot of fun shorty," he said, unable to control his self-grabbing a handful of her hair and pulling it to his cock. Kia opened her mouth and sucked it down halfway. June held her head and fucked her face. When she couldn't take it Kia pulled back for air and a long string of precum and spit connect them together. She took two deep breaths before attacking him again. Kia was a freak and he understood how she got what she wanted from man. He pulled back on the break of nutting and told her to get up on the bed. Kia did what she was instructed and lay on her back. He got between her legs and slowly began to slide inside her. Her mouth was open, and she moaned. "Shit, shiiit," she said as he pushed inside her. He felt unbelievably good. He began to go in and out taking her to heaven. "Boy who taught you to fuck like this?" She asked out of breath. This turned him on more. Making him go faster. June was lost in the moment the cat was so good he had to hold off from nutting too soon. Kia felt him hitting her spot and closed her eyes." Damn that's it, stay right there!" She yelled cumming once more. While in the middle of her orgasm June pulled out and dove down to taste her Goode's. He sucked at her clit until she couldn't take it. When she relaxed, he got up kissed her allowing her to taste the treat. Kia sucked on his lips loving how she taste. June slid his whole pole in her and one quick struck take her breath away. He stood up still inside her and fucking her harder while holding her in the air. Kia placed her hands on his shoulder while he pounded her insides. After a few minutes he put her down and fucked her for another 40 minutes.

Afterwards Kia lay settled in bed sweating and satisfied. June perched on the edge of the mattress putting on his boxer. "Can you get me some weed?" He asked. Kia got up and stood in front of him. "I can get you anything you want." She said. Dropping to her knees and grabbing ahold of his tool. "But first you owe me another hour," she added. *Damn this bitch a freak.* June thought.

Kia stood to her feet, "let's do it in the shower this time," she said walking into the bathroom. June chuckled he'd never met a woman with a higher sex drive than his.

Chapter Nine

* * * * *

T he layout of the office was as nice as any fortune 500 CEO's would be. Anyone who entered would assume it belonged to a legitimate businessman. It was well kept and orderly, from the staff continuously cleaning. Bee stood beside her father, behind his desk as he had a meeting with his accountant. She been attached to him at the hip the last few days just taking in game. He was a great leader and even better businessman. She was studying how to take over the family empire. Bee wasn't really the one for numbers and this meeting wasn't one she wanted to attend. She kissed her father on the head and whispered in his ear, she'd be in her room. Danjunema didn't respond, too caught up in the money to care. Bee didn't take it personally knowing how he got when money was being discussed.

When Bee made it to her room, she closed the door, and drop on the bed. She appreciated being around her family but missed being around people her own age. She missed the friendship she had with Black and Glory, but that was a thing of the pass, something she'd have to let go. She wanted to have some fun. And thought about going clubbing but quickly dismissed the idea. She was horny but not ready to fuck yet. She pounded her face against the bed, before getting up. "Fuck" she yelled. Frustrated, she couldn't find nothing pleasant to get into. A moment later there was a light knock on the door before Danjunema pushed it open. "I'm gone to interrogate a disloyal employee, you wanna come?" Danjunema asked. This was right up her Alley. "I wouldn't miss it for nothing in the world." She said. Danjunema looked at his child, with mixed emotions. She was a demon, and he liked it and disliked it at the same time. One thing for sure she had his blood flowing through her veins. "Well meet me downstairs in 5 minutes," he said, as he turned to leave. "Can I be the one asking the questions?" She asked hoping to get a chance to cause some pain. "We'll see!" He said knowing she wouldn't be denied. Bee wasn't one for number, but murder was her game. She couldn't wait for this opportunity to torcher someone. Hopefully, it was as entertaining as it looked in movies. Bee got her things and walked downstairs to wait in the car for her father. When she made it to the motor vehicle the driver opened the door for her, and she jumped in. She picked up her phone and went on Facebook, people where still screaming RIP Cash. It was getting on her nerves. In her eyes he was a lame. She was glad he was gone. Bee clicked on his picture and though he was a handsome man. While she was looking at the picture her father got the vehicle, he noticed her viewing Cash picture. "Why are you looking at that?" He asked. Bee didn't have a answer for the question, so she surged her shoulders. "I did that for you. You never leave unfinished business." He said. Bee raised her eyebrows; this was brand new information. "Why you never told me you had him murder?" She asked as they pulled off heading to her destination. " I've had lots of people killed in my life, its nothing to over think." He said nonchalantly. Bee admired how he carried his self.

She eyed the picture once more but in a different light this time." So, when we get there, I don't want you to go overboard right away. I want you to start slow. I'm gone ask him a few questions. If I like the answers, we let him go if not you get to have some fun." He said. Bee rubbed her hands together. " what he do? I wanna know so I could start thinking of his punishment?" She asked, taking her lesson seriously, and wanted all the details beforehand.

"Short answer is he cost me 2 million." Danjunema said like it was nothing. " how can you say that like it ain't nothing? " she asked wanting to know how he could be so clam.

"It's only money to me now, but there was a time when playing with my money could get your whole family killed. So, it take time. The more money you have the less inconvenient it is if you lose some." he said looking out the window. Bee sat quiet the rest of the ride, just thinking about what techniques to use on her victim. They pulled up to an abandon apartment on the south side of Chicago before packing. Bee followed her dad inside in down to the basement. A man set naked, beating, and tied to a chair. Bee smiled unable to control her emotions. She couldn't wait to get down to business. There was a seat placed in front of the naked man. Which her father took, she stood behind him again but this time a lot more interested. Danjunema sat there quickly just starring at the batter man, this mouth was duck taped so he couldn't say a word, but it didn't stop him from mumbling. Bee had enough of the silent game and walked over and pulling the duct taped from his mouth.

Her dad looked at her with murder in his eyes. "What I'm ready to play!" She said and a childish voice. A smile spread across his face, *she was something else,* he though. "I'm sorry for her impatience, but she's really looking forward to her first interrogation. But something tells me she's a natural..... But this is how things are going to work. I'm gone ask you a few questions if you lie, she gets a shot at you." He said. Bee waved in blow him a kiss. The man looked at her pretty face before looking into her cold eyes. "If you tell the truth you leave here unharmed." Danjunema continued.

The man couldn't wait to tell his story, and they listened as he told them how he'd been robbed while driving the truckload of product. At the conclusion of this story, it was clear he had nothing to do with the robbery. Bee was disappointed the longer he spoke. She really wanted him to be dishonest so she could get blood on her hands. Danjunema stood up in walked over to the man. He smacked his face lightly, "you did the right thing, by telling me the truth. It wouldn't cause you a lotta pain to lie." Danjunema said walking over to Bee. The disappointment was all over her face. "Damn I was praying you'd lie so my child could have some fun. Now you left me between a rock and a hard place. On one hand, I want to keep my word, and let you go, on the other I don't wanna disappoint my baby girl. " he said.

"Come on man I did what you asked." The man yelled. Bee bit her bottom lip try'na hold back her wishes, but she was unsuccessful. "just let me shoot him then, once in the head it will be quick. He won't feel a thing," she said through pleading eyes.

"Okay, make sure you shoot him between the eyes." Danjunema said, giving in.

"No please," the man begged. Bee had her pistol out in a split second. She walked over to the man who was crying and begging. Bee placed the gun to his forehead. She was the happiest she'd been in days at that moment.

Boom!

She pulled the trigger, blowing his brains out. The force of impact knocked over the chair. Blood slapped on her face and lips and she licked it off loving the taste.

* * * * *

Marvell's life was amazing in his young eyes' things couldn't get better. The things the game blessed him with, and such a short period made him feel like the chosen one. It was like he could do no wrong when it came to the hustle, every move he made was profitable.

But Marvell wasn't let it go to his head he'd become humbler since having money, than when he was broke.

This relationship with his mother was constantly improving. They went out to eat and just laughed like old times. His made him feel good inside which only made him hustle harder to get her off Allied. The trap phone was doing about 4 bands a day and it was good. But right now, he was relaxing inside his car with an 18-year-old hood rat he'd had a crush on for years. It was crazy how money could give you the opportunity you'd only dreamed of. Before hustling he could only image a chance at having her company. Now here she was in his passenger seat smiling and laughing at everything he said like he was Kevin Heart. He planned on getting his first shot of pussy tonight. In by the looks she was giving him it was already in the bag.

"Marvell I'm hungry." She said, testing to see if he was cheap. He looked at the Jordon Woods look alike and had no problem with getting her a meal.

"What you try'na get?" He asked. Turning the engine on, to pull out the lot. He looked up at his apartment and saw his momma starring down at him. She smiled happy to see her son with a woman.

"I don't know... Let go to my house and order something." She said. Marvell gave it his all to play it cool, "say know mo," he said pulling off. She only lived a half block awhile, so it only took second to get to her apartment. When she stepped out, he looked at her ass and prayed he didn't make a fool of his self-tonight. But he just planed on doing what he saw in porn move and hopefully that would be enough. They made it inside and he took a seat, while Lisa was on the phone ordering pizza. When she was done placing their order, she came over and took a seat next to him. She noticed he was nervous and wondered if he'd ever had sex before. Lisa saw him around but never once with a girl. She glanced at him he was handsome, but she never paid him any attention until now.

"Stop staring!" He said a little uncomfortable.

"Can I ask you a question." She said scooting closer to him and placing a hand on his leg.

"What to it?" He responded.

"Don't take this the wrong way. Why I never seen you with a girl friend?" She asked.

"Shit I'm gone keep it hot with you. It's cause I never had one." He said not being one to lie. Lisa rises her eyebrows; she was right to assume he was a virgin.

"You a virgin? " she asked, turned on at the thought of being able to show him the ropes. Marvell thought about lying for a second but believed she'd be able to tell once they had sex.

"Hell ya," he said putting his head down ashamed. Lisa lifted his head with her hands. "Well, that's about to change," she said taking him by the hand to her room.

* * * * *

June sat with Kutta, Bullet, and Black at her kitchen table passing around a few blunts. They'd be staying with her while in Madison. Kutta wanted to tell June what happened in Chicago but hadn't gotten around to it. He didn't trust Black after they kidnapped her. But June seemed to trust her enough to stay with her. June since how they never talked around Black but didn't want to be ordering her around in her home. He stood up and asked to speak to her quick in the back. Black followed him to her room and closed the door behind her. June turned to face her, "a Black, I ain't try'na tell you what to do in yo shit., but if you can chill back here while I talk to my boys?" He asked. Black put her hand on her hips and frond, before smirking." Boy I ain't one of them funny acting hoe's if you need privacy it yours," she said sitting on the bed.

"Cool good looking," he said turning to leave.

"First let me get one of them blunts" Black said. June went and got her one before going back up front. He was tired as hell after going a few rounds with Kia sexy ass. The meet for the pounds went well, and Kia would have them soon. So, Black would be able to get some money herself. It made him feel great to help her.

"What happened now skud?" He asked taking a set.

"You trust that bitch?" Kutta asked.

"Ya, she good people! She ain't got nobody, so she rocking with us." He said. Kutta and Bullet looked lost, but let it go. June's judgement was good enough for them.

"So, look skud, long story short the old head said Cash was a nobody. He was the real boss nigga. He even said ain't shit gone change, and anybody with you gone get hit as well." Kutta said.

"Look bro them nigga had that bitch let up like they was addressing a congregation of some shit. Them nigga's look like real soldiers bro." Bullet said.

"They want you gone bad, and I think them old head ain't got a problem laying on you, until it's done. I don't think you gotta worry about the rest of the guys as much as you need to worry about them" Kutta added. June didn't say a word just listened. He remembered Cash confided in him about these old school Dell Viking niggaz he knew, and June wondered, if that's who they were referring to. One thing for sure he needed to get ahead of this thing before it cost him his life.

"Bro why don't you just let them know you ain't have shit to do with it?" Bullet asked. June looked at him like he'd lost his mind. "How can I prove it? They ain't gone wanna hear shit I say. When they see me, it gone be nothing but gun smoke. " June said. Bullet put his head down and started brainstorming other ideas, it came up with nothing. "look we just gotta stay alert and get this outta town money. Then we put cash on they head." Kutta said.

June hit the weed thinking long and hard for a while." I know how to get it done bro." He said a little louder than necessary." I been fucking this bitch, who husband getting money in the city. He from Africa, the biggest Kingpin in the city. The plan is we kidnap her and make it seem like it's a hit from the BD's. This should start a war in the city and keep things off us for a while. If the Africans win, we free to move on our own. If not at lease we bought ourselves some time." June added.

"So you wanna kidnap another bitch ?" Bullet asked, sarcastically.

"Ya!" June responded.

"Ion know bro, the last bitch we kidnapped still around months later." Kutta added.

"Look bro this our only chance. We gotta do this to get them off our ass for a while. If not, we ain't gone be able to hide long." June said.

"Fuck it then!" Kutta said passing the blunt.

"When we gone do this?" Bullet asked.

"Ion know, whenever she calls me again. But until then we gotta get as much work off as possible. I wanna grab enough coke to last until they pay the ransom. When they do we let her go and continue to do business as usually. This how we win. Gotta outthink niggas!" He said. The more he ponders on it the better it seemed to him. He only had a few things to hash out before they carried it out. One thing was figuring out how do they blame the guys for the kidnapping. But he had a while to get that together right now he needed to focus on dumping the rest of his product.

Black sat in her room while June and his friends talked. She was thinking about getting money. With June protection the sky was the limit. She discovered the supply of loud took a hit with Bee's missing in action. She was searching to fill that void in get rich in the meantime. Black was worried about Bee and hope you was somewhere safe instead on in a grave. It didn't matter if they, were no longer friends, she'd never wish harm one her. Life took them in different direction, but they'd always be kin. Black got up she was going for a ride. When she walked into the kitchen the room fell silent. "Can I use your car," she asked. June threw her the keys and she left. She got in the vehicle and pulled off. Black turned on the music, and just relaxed her mind. She was about to begin a new journey and become her own boss.

This scared her a little bit, because she always been a follower and did what others instructed. She wounded if she had what it took? She hated his part of herself, the part that didn't believe, and always stood in her way. Her low self-esteem was well hiding from others with jokes, but she couldn't hide from herself. *You got this.* She thought. Black pulled up to the club she used to own with her friends. The place looked like a ghost town. The parking lot once packed with cars was empty. It had not opened for mouths. Black though about getting it back up and running and smiled. *Ya that's what I'm gone do!* She said to herself before pulling off with a new purpose. Black planned on making it bigger and better this go around. The name would be Glory's nightclub in memory of her lost sister.

* * * * *

Kia made it home late that night and found her husband in bed sleep. She went to Bee room and she was sound asleep as well. They both look like they'd run themselves down to the bone. Knowing Danjunema there was no telling the kind of lessons Bee learned today. She could only guess it was something worthwhile. Kia went back downstairs and took a seat on the couth before turning on the news. It was the same shit as always murder and mayhem. She closed her legs in her pussy reminded her of the beating June put her through a few hours ago. The boy was amazing in bed something outta this world. She just hoped he didn't end up dead like the last couple of good lovers she'd found. Kia wasn't slow though she knew the chances of that was very high with the lifestyle he lived. If he was killed, she'd just replace him no big deal. It wasn't any emotions evolved just fucking. Something she'd become accustom to since Angel and Money.

She planned to call him next week and get some more. But first she needed to place his order for the loud. At the moment she realized she'd left the 300,000 and the car, *fuck it I'll get it in the morning,* she thought. Kia went in the kitchen to make her a late-night snack before going to bed. She retrieved some bread and meat and quickly made a sandwich and cut it in half before taking a seat at the table. She looked around her house just amazed at how far she'd come. It wasn't long ago she was shacking her ass at a nightclub. It felt good to have everything she'd dream of. Her luck finally turned around and she was living the dream. The world was hers and she took full advantage of being a queen pin. It felt great treating men like they did women. The power she had over them was intoxicating. But the effect was light compared to what she felt when she looked at her bank account. She was worth more than she'd ever dreamed. Kia heard light footsteps before Bee enter the kitchen hold a firearm in her left head." Oh, it just you!" Bee said to her mother. Kia looked at her, you don't need that baby..... That's what we pay the soldiers for." Kia said hoping to ease her fears. Bee took a set across from her place the gun on the counter before saying, " I rather have it and not need it, then to need it and not having it," she said. Kia respected, that and left it alone. "Can't sleep" she asked.

"Nah, I heard noise, and wanted to make sure nobody was down here." She said picking up the other half of the sandwich and taking a bight." Can I ask you something? " Kia asked.

"Anything!" Bee responded.

"Why you so trigger happy?" Kia asked, hoping she didn't offend her. Bee thought about if for a second. She wondered this herself, the only thing that came to mind was the rush she got from taking a soul.

"When I got my first couple bodies I was hooked. It just puts me at ease when I take a life, and makes me god, if only for a second, I'm not a lost soul I'm the deliver." She said smirking.

Kia felt the hairs on the back of her neck stand up. Bee noticed the look, and stood to leave," I'm going to bed!" She said leaving kia speechless.

* * * * *

Black woke up to the sound of laugher in the front room. She heard June cracking jokes with his friends, before getting up to go take a shower. Once she was in the water she relaxed as the water washed over her. When she made it home, they were sleeping about an hour later June came and slept with her.

Black got out the shower and got dressed. When she entered the living room, they were dressed; June was looking good as hell she thought. He wore a white, red, and green Gucci shirt. Some badge, red and green Gucci shoe's and a badge bucket hat. His jeans were blue in his belt matched his hat and shoe's. When June saw her, and said," I got good news for you." Pulling her to the back again. "I got the pounds ready for you. They want us to pick them out tonight. I guess they got different kinds." He said. Black smiled glad to get the news. At the moment her phone ringed and she picked it up. June walked back up front giving her privacy. A minute later he heard black calling his name. "What's up with all this back in forward shit." Kutta asked "what you'll got going on we can't know about?" He asked.

"Mine yo business!" June teased and walked into black room. It was her turn to have good news for him," I got somebody who want to get 3 of them off you." She said.

"When? Like right now!" He asked.

"Ya he said he need em like yesterday."

"Shit call that nigga back and tell him to link" June said excited. Black made the call and they set up the meeting on the North side. June told Kutta to follow behind them and to fan the nigga down if anything happened. Black assured them he wasn't the type of dude to rob them, but they knew better to believe that. Anybody could turn into a robber if times were hard enough. The game ain't have no rules now-a-days. So called thugs and killers would set they man's up, one moment kill, them and rat the next moment. Shit was just outta hand with the new school.

30 minutes later they arrived on Kipling and pulling in the lot. Kutta and Bullet got out the car and post up on both ends of the parking lot. Black watched how prepared they were and said,

"Y'all stay on point! "June looks out the window as the black Chevy pulled into the lot. " It's either be on point or be in a grave. " he said. Keep his eyes on the car. When it stopped and packed, he went and got in the passenger side with the duffle bag. Bullet monitored the parking lot while Kutta turn to face the Chevy. A minute later June hoped out and the Chevy pulled out the lot. Black watched in amazement at how down pack they had their system. June got in the car with her and pulled off slowly Black noticed him watching the rearview mirror, so she glanced back and saw Kutta trailing them while bullet walked alone side the car. When they pulled out the lot, she saw Bullet finally got inside the cars. "He ain't get in until we pulled out incase somebody ambush us. It's easier to shoot from outside the car then in it." He said reading her mind. She was really impressed by them. Black phone ring again it was the customers they'd just left.

"Hello!" She said.

"I'm gone give you another call later tonight I only grabbed a few to make sure it wasn't a let up. " he said.

"Boy, I don't play them type of games" she responded.

"It better safe than sorry." He said. Black told him to just call and they'd make it happen. She related the news to June who just shook his head. Seeing him making moves had Black prepared to get on her grind.

Chicago

3 men sat inside a small sandwich shop playing poker and sipping lightly on fine wine. Strick the leader of the gang was winning big time, not because of skill, but because the others was afraid of what might happen if he lost. Strick was an old school Dell Viking who turned to BD back on 35th when they all flapped. He put in so much work as a youngest that he rose to the top and before long he became the new king. He used his street smarts and never truly claimed the crown, to avoid a reco indictment. He didn't want the fame just the money and power. He'd appointed Cash in the spot to run things for him and felt personally responsible for revenging is murder. He got up from the table after winning another hand and walked to the back room where his staff was packaging his product. The sandwich shop was only a front for what was really going on. In the back room where all the finest firearms anyone could get their hands on, alone with some coke. The coke wasn't the best, so he gave Cash the freedom to push his own, as long as he gave tin present to the BD and brought his gun from them as well. Cash didn't have a problem with his arrangement, so business was great between them. Strick went into the bathroom and took a piss before returning to the poker game. As he sat 3 plain clothes officers' step into the chambers. Strick looked up at them before waving for the other player to leave the room, which they did. The cops took a seat, "What can we do for you boss," one asked.

"I need to locate someone ASAP." Strick said, passing them a folded with all June information inside. One of the officers peeked inside noticing the picture, "isn't this one of yo boi?" He asked. Strick took a pull from his back wood and blew it in the officer face." Just do as your told you don't get paid to ask questions. Well at lease not by me." She said placing 20,000 on the table. The officers glanced at the Cash before taking it," You right boss! We will have something for you by the end of the week." One said before they stood. " Ya you do that!" Strick said, waving them off, and they left the room. Strick hated doing business with them, but it's a necessary evil. They were the reason he'd never spent a day in jail. He also had them worn Cash of any investigations on him and his team. With them by his side he was one step ahead of the law. They were also very useful and other ways as well; he knew they'd have June location and know time in deliver June to him alive. He plans on cutting June's hands of in front of the whole crew to show them what happen to those who bit the hand that fed them. Then after that he'd have June buried alive. The loss of Cash forced him to find someone to take the crown while he played the background. It wouldn't be easy to find a strong successor, to replace a man who become beloved amongst the people. But it needed to be done to keep the heat off him. As long as the team felt they was taking orders from him this freedom was on the line.

Two days later

June and Black sat at a hotel with Kia deliveryman going through the different types of loud they could choose from. Black was in business mold, but June was thinking bout trying some of the smoke once they were done. He was like a kid in a Candy store. Black shook her head at him he was smiling hard as hell. "You okay?" She asked June. He shook his head, unable to take his eyes away from the smoke. Black picked 3 different types knowing they wasn't available in Madison and would sell quick. They were informed it would be delivered to them tonight. June bought a few samples to take with him he couldn't wait until later. As soon as they were in the automobile, he started to roll a blunt. "Boi you a weed head." Black said taking off. " tell me something I don't know!" He said breaking the blunt down. Over the last few days June had sold all but 3 bricks. Things were going well but he hoped they picked up a little more. They were out gunning for him, and something was telling him they were getting close. At times it felt like someone was watching him and he wasn't able to shack the feeling.

Black arrived at the apartment and they made their way inside. They walked in the house and Kutta and Bullet was still sleeping. Black went back to her room as June blow the loud in Bullet face. Bullet woke up, "what's that?" He asked, putting his hand out for the blunt. June past it to him," I don't even know the name of this shit!" June said," but taste it, that shit hitting just right." He added. Bullet smacked his lips together. "ya this that move," he said hitting it a few more times. "What's that," Kutta asked smelling the loud waking him up. Bullet passed it to him, which he took two big pulls from." Black walked in the room and saw them smoking the weed and said, "y'all some nasty nigga's, ain't even brushed ya teeth and smoking. " she said only halfway joking.

"Man fuck all that I smelled this shit and had to hit it." Kutta said. Black laughed at him, "y'all hungry? " she asked. "Hell ya," bullet said going to the bathroom to take care of his hygiene. "What about y'all two," she asked Kutta and June. They said yes, so she headed to the kitchen to make some pancakes.

June loved how consistent Black was, she wasn't one of them funny acting bitches. She woke up the same way she went to sleep cool as a fan. She'd grown on Bullet in Kutta within a few days and they treat her like family. She really just fit in with ease, nothing was forced. June strolled up behind Black in kissed her lightly on the back of the neck pulling her close to him. "When you gone give me some mo of this pussy?" He asked. Black felt his hard dick press against her ass. She bottled her eyes in moaned." You could've had it the last few nights you slept in my bed. You just didn't make a move!" She said pressing her ass against him harder. "What y'all on in here?" Bullet asked walking in on them and taking a seat at the table. "None of yo business!" Black said as June released her and took a seat. She finished cooking the food just as Kutta enter the kitchen after brushing his teeth and wishing his face. She made them all a plate before preparing one for herself and they all sat at the table eating. "So Black how long was you fucking with Cash?" Bullet asked putting some food in his mouth. Black stopped eating, "not long maybe a few mouths." She said.

"So, you like girls too?" He asked.

"What made you say that?" She asked.

"Cause I heard that's how Cash like em" he said. June eyed Bullet like he'd lost his mind.

"I guess I do. Well, I've only done it a few times, but I did like it." She said honestly.

"See this a good woman right here. Most female would've lied about this shit, try'na make they self look innocent. But she didn't think twice just keep it real." Bullet said.

"Look I ain't ashamed of nothing I did. So, I don't have to lie." She said.

June jumped in to switch the subject before Bullet went full blow match maker on them. "So, we gotta bust this move for two of them things, then we gone reup I don't see the point in waiting too much longer." He said. Bullet noticed what he was doing but let it go. Money was more important than his personal entertainment. He was getting a kick outta making June uncomfortable. His game of match maker wasn't just all fun in games either, he wanted to see June move on him from the loss of Kim. He had a front row seat at how much it scared June and wanted the best for his brother. Bullet knew Black would never replace Kim in his heart, but it would be a start at healing his soul. "What time we gotta head out?" Kutta asked with a mouth full of food. "In a couple hours," June said. Rubbing Black's thigh under the table. She starred in his eyes. He was really turning her on, and he saw it in her eyes. "Damn why don't y'all just go in the back in get that shit over with." Bullet joked aware of the sexy tension in the air. Black licked her lips at June, "how bout it." She said glancing in his eyes. Instead of answering June stood up and went to the back. Black quickly followed him out the room. Bullet and Kutta sat at the table for about 5 minutes before black moans could be heard. She was so loud, they both looked over at each other wide eyed. "A skud let's hit the mall up." Kutta said. He wanted a new fit and to try to bump a bitch." Ya let's get up outta here." Bullet said because Black moan was starting to turn him on. They got up and left the house as they jumped in the vehicle Bullet spotted two white dudes peeking into June car. "A bro fuck you looking for?" He asked clinching his 9mm. Kutta saw Bullet approach the dudes and step out the car.

Bloc!

He heard a gunshot and ducked low grabbing his pistol from off his hip. A screeching car sped out the lot. Kutta turn the corner and saw bullet laying on the floor pistol in his hand a single shot to the forehead. He walked over to his best friend with tears in his eyes. Kutta dropped to his knee's grabbing the pistol outta his hand and closed his eyes. "What the fuck happen!" June said running into the parking lot buttoning up his pants with Black close behind him. They'd heard the gunshot from the apartment and rushed downstairs. Kutta couldn't find words, he sat there in shock. June looked at him with questioning eyes. "We gotta go!" Black said because the police would be there any moment. June took off running to the car, and Black followed. Kutta sat at the side of his best friend unable to move. "Come on skud..." June yelled. Kutta slowly walked over to the car trying to hand June 2 pistols. "take these with you skud I can't leave his body out here." Kutta said. June glared into his eyes, " We gotta go, ain't shit you can do for him now bro. Going to jail ain't gone help none." June said with pleading eyes. Kutta thought about it and slowly got in the back seat. As June pulled off, they passed Bullet body and Kutta starred at it and whispered, "I'm sorry skud." As tears poured from his eyes. June exited the lot and a block away they passed police rushing to the seen. "What happened back there?" June asked. Black turn in looked at Kutta when he didn't respond.

He had his head low looking at the blood on his hands. "He in shock." Black said to June.

June peeked in the rearview mirror and saw Kutta shaking. He'd never seen him this visibly shaking and decided to ask him questions once they were somewhere safe. June thought about the bricks at Black house and pray to god they didn't link them to her apartment if so, the feds would be looking for her soon. "Man, I hope 12 don't run in yo house and find them bricks." He said. Glad he'd decided to leave this cash in the trunk of the car. He could take the lost on the work, but at this point he couldn't afford a financial lost in the dollars department. Black didn't want them to search her apartment but wasn't worried about it being linked to her. When she first moved in, she got it under an alias because she was underaged at the time. "It doesn't matter that place ain't in my name. The real issue is the building has cameras everywhere they have the murder on tape, as well as everything we've done outside my apartment." She said as she tried to remember if she'd done anything illegal on tape. She quickly ruled that out for herself before asking, "you wasn't meeting people out there?" She asked.

"Nah, I wouldn't disrespect yo crib like that!" He said as he got on the expressway headed to Beloit. They needed to get outta town until they found out what the police new. June looked in the back Kutta was still staring at his hands. June really prayed he'd be ok. He'd been really close with bullet since childhood. June knew from personal experience losing someone that close, could fuck with you mentally." You good bro?" He asked, but Kutta didn't respond. Black turned around in her seat. She touched Kutta hand causing him to jump and grabbed his Glock 9 on his hip. Black jumped backward putting her hands up. Kutta saw her and removed his hand from his firearm and put his head down. June watched them, "just let him get his mind right." He told Black who turned around in her seat shocking up. She feared he needed help but didn't say anything.

Kutta looked at his hand as the memoir of what happened played over and over in his head. One-minute Bullet was ok the next he was gone. Thing happened to quickly and Kutta though hard on what he could've done differently to save his brother but kept coming up empty. He wondered how they were able to get a jump on Bullet but would never know. He laid his head back and closed his eyes, Bullet was slaughtered on his watch, something that would weight heavy on him forever.

June looked in the mirror again and was glad to see Kutta no longer staring at his hands. It was a sign that his mind was still processing things. When they made it to Beloit, he'd ask what happened again. Black placed her hand on his lap and rubbed it letting him know she was there for him. June mustered up a weak smile and held her hand. "This street shit to much at times." He said shaking his head.

"I know. It's crazy how the game plays out. It's like this shit is stacked against us. You play but you never win." Black said upset.

* * * * *

Strick phone rang while he was in his backyard play with his children. "Daddy will be right back." He said answering and walking away.

"What?" He said upset someone interrupt him on family day.

"We have a problem." One of the law enforcement officers said. Strick looked at the phone again, " I pay you to fix problems not have em!" He yelled causing his son to look over and lower his hands indicating for him to be quiet. Strick shook his head letting his son feel he was in control. " I know boss, but something went wrong.... We need to meet with you ASAP. " Strick was already upset about the interruption, now he was ferrous. "Meet me at the sandwich shop." He said ending the conversation. He walked over to his kids and told them it was time to go inside. They put up a fuss, but he convinced them he'd take them shopping in the morning. An hour later he pulled up to the sandwich shop. He made his way inside where the two-officer sat in the back alone with a few of his man. Strick cleared out the room leaving him and the officers. "What happened." He said taking a seat. They looked to each other, wondering who'd tell him the bad news.

 The taller one chose to speak, "We found the offender, and was looking insid-"

"What fucking offender? I asked y'all to find June not some sex offender" he said not understanding the choice of words.

"Oh, I'm sorry. I meant we found June and was peeking in his car, when two other man saw us. One approached us with a firearm, and we had to use deadly forces." He said.

"What that's got to do with me?" Strick asked confused.

"This happened on video. Its on camera, we were in the process of breaking into his car, when we were confronted. When they find out it's us, we'll be arrested and are badges took." He continued.

"I see... What I'll do is put y'all up in one of my hideouts until we get more information." He said already plotting their demise. They knew too much, to be arrested.

"Thank you!" The other one said.

"No problem. Wait here I'll give my team instructions on where to take y'all" he lied getting up and leaving the room. Once he was up front, he whispered to his top commando," Kill them and get rid of the car and body's. Make sure you leave no truce of them ever being in this building. " he said before walking out and getting in his car to head home.

He really needed to find a replacement for Cash. It was too demanding being back in the management position. He liked it better when he was just the owner from afar.

* * * * *

June pulled up and parked the car outside the hotel. Black went in and got them a room before they followed her inside. Once they were in the space Kutta went straight to the bathroom to take a shower. June ran to the clothing store to get him a change of clothes. When he walked back in Black sat on one of the double beds just staring off in space. She looked at him when he entered. " He still in the shower?" He asked Black. She shook her head yes. June knocked on the door," A skud I got you some clothes. " June said, before slightly opening the door and putting the outfit on the sink. "Good looking!" Kutta said. June released a deep breath. It was music to his eyes to here Kutta talking. He thanked god he was alright. June went and sat next to Black, she took his hand, in held it tight. "I been losing people all my life, and the fucked-up part is I'm becoming numb to the pain." He said shaking his head." I hate it had to be this way, sometimes I ask god why cause this shit is too much at time. I ask him why we were born into poverty and had to go up on the streets. This shit ain't fare. We didn't do nothing to deserve this lifestyle. We were just born into it" He said getting a little emotional. Black looked at him, before saying, " June you know you could walk away from this at any time. You could start a business and just live a normal life. You got money now. The only thing keeping you in the game is you." She said being honest with him." June thought about what she'd said, it was 100% true. " I got some money but it ain't enough, plus niggas try'na get me killed. Just because I say I'm done don't mean the streets gone let me walk away. Not after all the shit I did." June said.

Kutta walked out the bathroom interrupting their conversation. He sat down across from him and rubbed his hands over his face as they watched him. "I'm sorry skud!" He said finally looking at June.

"Come on skud that shit could've happen to any of us. Now tell me what happened. Kutta ran the story off to them as he could remember." So, they was looking in my shit?" June asked confused.

"Ya!" Kutta said still try'na make it make since. He was just as confused as anyone. The whole things felt weird, it was something missing he just didn't know what.

"You think that was the guys try'na get me killed?" June asked.

"Nah the shooters were white boys. I don't think the guys coming like that." Kutta said.

"White boi's" Black asked. Kutta shook his head still thinking things over. He couldn't come up with anything. "Bro they looked like 12! Undercover officers " he said as he remembered the car. It was tinted out and had the bumper cop cars have in the front.

"Nah it couldn't be 12 they wouldn't have fled the scene." June said. Kutta thought about it, "unless they on somebody pay role in was coming to kill you. " Kutta said making since of it all.

"Who we know got the law on the play role?" June asked suspicious of what he was hearing.

"Man, ain't know tell what them old heads into!" Kutta said with wide eyes. " The way that meeting was set up, it looked like some organized crime shit." He added. Black listened to them the more she heard the scared she became. Who the fuck was they beefing with? She wonders what she had gotten herself into running around with them, and for the first time since the kidnapping, she stated to plain her escape. "We gotta stop playing game and get back to Chicago and get these niggaz out the way." June said. Kutta glanced up at him and smiled for the first time." I thought you would never say it!" He said, wanting revenge from the loss of his friend. He didn't want to waste another second running. Kutta was ready to go on the offensive. Being hunted was his game he was used to being the one sliding not hiding. "So, when we leaving?" He added, hoping they left that moment. June looked at him and wondered if he understood what they were up against before saying, "in the morning."

* * * * *

Kia sat with her family out to eat, for their first family night. Thing was going great in their newly meant family. Other than their child being bloodthirsty. Kia talked to Danjunema about her concerns, but he said they all had blood on their hands. He told her not to judge, because she wasn't innocent. He put her at ease and ever since, they'd being enjoying the high life. "So, when are we gone take a trip to Africa?" Bee asked. She'd heard all about their last trip their and wanted to experience it on her own. "We can anytime you want." Danjunema answered, taking a sip of his wine. "I wanna go today. " Bee said filled with joy. Kia looked at her like, they couldn't leave that soon, she thought." Then today it is." Danjunema said placing his glass on the table. Kia shook her head before Bee was able to celebrate. "She needs a passport and I have business." Kia said.

"The passport is no big deal; I know a guy who owe me a favor. And one of my guys can take care of your business." Danjunema said.

Bee looked at Kia with pleading eyes. Kia didn't want to let them down, but she wasn't ready to leave the States. She treasured Africa but it wasn't home, and she just felt safer in America." I just can't go today! But y'all go ahead. " she said. Bee looked at her father hoping he didn't change his mind, "so can we still go?" She asked.

"Yes, we can I just gotta make a few calls to set everything up." He said. Bee jumped up and came around and hugged him. "Thank you," she said. Kia got up to use the bathroom, once she was alone, she called June. "Hello!" He answered.

"I need to see you again. My husband going outta town and I'm coming down there for a few days." She said without introducing herself.

"Cool say no more. A you know that move for them pounds? I need you to have yo people hold em until tomorrow and get me another 20 on the other side. I'm gone get em when I see you." He said.

"Will do." Kia responded before handing back to the table.

"We gotta get going to drop you off the jet will be waiting for us in an hour." Danjunema said.

"Last chance to change yo mind mom" Bee added.

"I wish, maybe next time." Kia lied; she didn't wish anything she was going where she desired the moment they left.

"It's her loss baby," Danjunema said, playing their bill before standing to leave. Kia followed them out to the limousine. They drove her home before heading out of the country. Kia marched into their residence, and the first thing she did was relieve all their staff, of their duties until Danjunema was home. Once she was alone, she went to take a shower. Kia quickly showered and got out, she noticed she had 3 missed calls from June. She phoned him back, and he informed her, they'd gather in Chicago instead of Madison. That was fine with her, it saved a two-hour drive. She got herself together and held out to the hotel. She checked in and relaxed watching TV until she heard a knock on the door an hour and a half later. She opened it and June walked in, smelling great and swagged out. " How you doing? " he asked. Walking in the room, it was nice, and one of Chicago 5star hotels called the Peninsula Chicago. June took a seat and one of the armchairs while Kia let the door locked behind him. "I'm blessed," she said, walking over in getting the bottle she'd order and poured them both a Glass. June took the drank and downed it. He had a lot on his mind at the moment. They were back I'm Chicago everyone but Black. She stayed in Beloit choosing to set this one out. He didn't blame her; they were on a mission which had almost no chance at success. June watched as Kia downed her drink, before refilling it. "Slow down ma, I ain't try'na get no pissy drunk pussy." June said. Kia looked at him, "I been doing this a long time. I know how to handle my liquor. " she said downing another glass." You got that" June said sipping on his glass. Over the next hour they made small talk while drinking. June was taking things cautiously, but Kia was pounding one after another and her lips became loose. June notice how open she was in decided to ask something he'd wondered a long time. "Why did you have Money killed?" Kia took another sip before" saying he played with my heart. I gave him chance after chance to be honest, but he wouldn't. So, I had him murdered." She laughed. June looked at her and saw a scorned woman. " You had him killed cause he cheated? " he asked. Kia stood to her feet and stumble before falling on the bed. " Yes and no. I had him killed because he couldn't be a man and man up for what he did." She said closing her eyes." He was a pussy just like this brother. " she said. June took out his phone to record the conversation to black mail her if need be in the future. He started the recording. "Damn shorty what you gotta against cash?" He asked. Kia opened her eyes, "He had my daughter shot, and put in a coma." She said, breaking out in laughter. June looked at her, she was a drunken mess. He promises to stop drinking after tonight. "He underestimated my baby and she live. My husband had him killed for his actions. "She said.

June was thunderstruck to hear this," what did you say?" He asked. Kia stood up and came to set on his lap, "My husband killed Cash!" She repeated.

"And who yo husband?"

"Danjunema!" She said kissing him on the lips. June returned her affection with joy. He was glad she'd given him the unexpected information. He picked her up and put her down on the bed. "I'm gone fuck the shit outta you." He said." But first I gotta use the bathroom." He added.

"Don't take too long," Kia said as she began to undress.

"I'll be right back," June said heading to the rest room. June walked in the bathroom and text Kutta. Skud I'm at hotel downtown. I'm leaving in the morning I want you to follow the bitch I walk out with to see where she stay. This shit could end the whole war. So, make sure you here. I'll text you again when we on our way out. June sent the text and flushed the toilet before washing his hands and heading back to the room. Kia was naked on the bed and he quickly undressed before calming on top of her. She reached down and grabbed his cock loving the feeling of it. She had him lay on his back and stroked his dick with two hands while looking up at him. June loves the way his big cock looked in her small hands. "Boy you're blessed." She said looking at his tool. "Tell me about it " June said, not referring to his package, but instead the information she'd giving him getting him out the hook for Cash murder. It was a blessing from god. Kia lined over and licked the precome from his cock. "Taste good too." She said.

June's thoughts were far away from the moment. Sex was the last thing on his mind, he couldn't wait to clear his name. Kia took him in her mouth and brought him back to the present with her skill." Damn ma you know how to suck the soul outta a nigga." He said. She pulled him from her mouth before saying, " you got one hell of a dick to suck." She said taking it down halfway. She sucked him until he was nice and hard before clamming on top of him and riding him over and hour, before falling asleep. June reclined in bed, he checked his phone and received a text from Kutta saying he'd be there. June fell asleep an hour later praying that his plan worked out.

* * * * *

The night was beautiful and the light from the moon light the block up. Inside his MC Marvell was recline with his hand on the back of Lisa had as she sucked him. She'd took his virginity, and he'd had her at his side since. Lisa enjoyed his company and didn't mind holding his work while he rode around hustling. Their arrangement was a win win. Marvell's phone was picking up every day. The money was rolling in and sometimes just to take a break he'd send her to make the serve. Marvell was liking having a companion to assist him with building and one like Lisa was the best. She'd suck and fuck him, and then get up at

3 in the morning to meet a customer. She took him deep in her month casing him to exploded. Lisa sucked it all down before releasing his dick. She sat up while Marvell put his pole back in his Gucci sweatpants.

You spending the night with me?" Lisa asked wanting to keep him under her.

"Hell ya! I just got meat TT real quick! He said picking up this phone to call him. TT answered the line," what good Tee?" He said while bagging up the have brick for Marvell.

"Where you want me to meet you?"

"I gotta bust a few moves so I'm gone come to you Tee. Meet me in yo momma lot!" He said hanging up the phone. Marvell and Lisa sat in the car playing music and talking. When his momma came to the car. He rolled the window down. "what up ma?" he asked.

"I need a few while I go over to your sister house. You know she been feeling down." She said. Marvell took a few bags out and give them to her." Here tell sis I love her!" He said. When his mother walked off Lisa asked." Why you give yo momma that shit! "

"She gone get high one way or another, so to stop people from taking advantage of her I make sure she don't need for nothing." He answered as TT pulled in the lot. He got out in go into TT whip, "what's good Tee?" He said going in his pocket pulling out the cash for the product. He handed it to TT, who gave him the half brick. " shit Tee try'na run it up," TT said. Marvell got the hint and hoped out. When he was back in the car, he handed the work to Lisa before going to her house.

Once they was inside they bagged up the work in dubs. It took them a few hours to do this, but Lisa didn't complain. She just liked being a part of something. Once they was done packaging everything Lisa went to the room and went to sleep, while Marvell stayed up watching TV, he got a text from this mother that really pissed him off. But he wasn't gone let it throw him off two much. There was nothing he could do about it so why worry.

At 12am he turned to 414 spotlight to watch Milwaukee local rappers. It was always very entertaining because you got to watch locals do their thing. His mind switched back to the news from his mom and hated how this shit always happen but if the chance came he'd do something about it.

Chapter Ten

* * * * *

Kia woke up with June still in her bed. She must have been drunk to allow him to say the night. Her head was banging. She tapped him on the shoulder," get up you gotta go!" She rudely said. June opened his eyes and noticed an expression of disguise on her face. "You gotta go!" She repeated. "I'll have 20 keys and that marijuana dropped off in an hour to the hotel in Beloit like you asked." She added, getting up and throwing him is clothes. June caught his jeans before they smacked him and the face. He laughed within knowing how it felt to be treated like a hoe. He put on his things as Kia sat holding the door open for him to leave. "I'll call you, when I get em." He said walking out the door.

Kia picked up the phone and ordered room service. Her head felt like it was gone explode. She couldn't remember much of what happened last night other than the business they'd discussed.

She called downstairs to room service and told them to place her food in the room before going to take a shower. After showing she ate her food and plan to go shopping before spending a few hours watching TV. The hotel phone ring and kia answered it and informed them she'd be checking out instead of staying another day. When she left the room, her spirit was high. The valet pulled up in her Range Rover and she tipped him before getting inside and pulling off. Her cell phone ring it was Bee.

"Hello," she answered.

"We made it ma. It's so beautiful here." Bee said amazed at the sight. Kia smiled remembering the experience. "I know it baby," Kia said making a left turn. "I wish you would've come with us." Bee said sincerely.

"I know baby I wish I was able to as well." Kia lied.

"Daddy want to speak with you." Bee said handing Danjunema the phone.

"Kia why did you let the whole staff off," Danjunema asked.

"I just wanted to be alone." She lied.

"Well, I like it when you at lease have a few guards on hand." He said. Danjunema hated how Kia didn't take security seriously. She went around like she was untouchable. When that was fare from the case. He knew at any moment anyone could be touched.

"I know but I can take care of myself." She said a little upset. She hated her husband tried treating her like a beginner in the game. She could handle her own. Or so she thought. Little did she know she was being followed.

* * * * *

174

June and Kutta followed behind Kia. After leaving the room he met Kutta downstairs and told him what Kia confessed to. Kutta was thunderstruck, by the revelation. This would get them off the hook for the murder and back into the skeem of things. They wouldn't have to worried about the BD's try'na kill them. June picked up his phone and called Devon.

Devon was from Cash hood; he'd be able to get June a council with the old head who was in control of things. From there June would tell them all he knew and hopes of getting in their good grace.

"Hello!" Devon answered.

"What good skud, this June."

"Fuck you calling my line for boi!" Devon said.

"Look skud-" June began but was cut off.

"Look bro, we ain't got shit to talk about. When I see you, I'm gone put you down, for that snake shit you pulled." Davon yelled in the phone.

"Ya all that. But I aint do that shit, but I know who did. I need you to link me up with the old head so I can show em that wasn't me." June said before Devon was able to hang up the phone.

"Skud em ain't taking know please pussy." Devon said.

"Look bitch ass nigga you tell them what I said or once I get in contact with them myself, I'm gone let em know I came to you first, and you wouldn't bring it to their attention." June said as he made a vile to kill Devon the moment he was back on the inside. Devon thought about it, withholding information about the murder could make it look like he was involved.

"Say know mo I'm gone call skud em,and let em know." He said, hanging up the phone in June's face.

"Bro I'm killing that nigga Devon," June said to Kutta.

"For what?" Kutta asked keeping his eyes on Kia Range Rover.

"The nigga was talking slick as hell like he on that." June laughed. He couldn't wait to clear his name once he did a lot of nigga's was getting put down for disrespecting it.

"Dude ain't on shit." Kutta said following Kia as she entered the mall parking lot.

They parked a few cars away from her and watched as she exited and entered the mall. "You want me to follow her inside?" Kutta asked scared to lose her. "Nah skud she gotta come back for the car. We just gone keep our eyes on it." June said taking out a blunt and lighting it up. Just as his phone ring, "What's up?" He asked Devon.

"Skud wants to meet at his sandwich shop tonight. I gave him this number he gone call you with more information. " Devon said hanging up in June face once more. "Bitch as nigga," June said placing the phone on this lap. "I gotta meet the nigga tonight." June added. Kutta looked at him confused, "fuck you mean you gotta meet with him?" He asked. Unwilling to allow June to go alone. June predicted his reaction and was ready with a response, "Look I know I might be walking into a trip, and I'm cool with that. But if you go with me, we both dead, and then who gone revenge us? I'm going in alone. If I don't come out, you know who to go after. " he said. Kutta thought it over, if he sat outside, he'd be able to identify anybody who left that shop. "Say no mo if you ain't outta there in an hour I'm coming inside shooting that bitch up." He said seriously. June passed him the blunt. "I already know."

* * * * *

June walked into the sandwich shop and was stopped at the door by a tall bodyguard. He scanned the room it was packed, with all eyes on him. He began to second guess his decision, but he manned up, if it was his time he'd die like a man. He thought over this plan as he was patted down. An older man who fit the description Kutta described walk in the room from the back. "Follow me." He said in a deep voice. June glance around again before following him to the back. They walked and the kitchen, and June scanned the room anticipating an ambush, but they were alone. The old man turned to face him," what evidence you got to clear yo name?" He asked as the door behind June opened. June understood whoever enter the room was there to pull the trigger if need be. June stood firm, " I know the name of cash's killer!" He asked staring the man in the eyes. "I'll give it to you but my name gotta be cleared, and I want Cash's spot at the top of the table." June added. Strick walked up close to him almost noise to noise. "You ain't running shit in here lil nigga, ion give a fuck about yo body count. I killed more nigga's in 96 then you killed yo whole life." He said, as a pistol was placed to the back of June neck. " I know I ain't running shit boss, I'm just playing the game to the fullest, even if it's my last play. I know you need a face, in I'm a face they respect. Once you clear my name, they'll fall in line behind me, and I'll be the go between them in you." She said. Strick thought about it a second, Cash filled him in on June a while ago, Cash was grooming June to take his place, from day one. Cash informed him of how smart June was, how he was a born leader. "If you got proof the spot yours." Strict said, taking a step back. June reached in his pocket in retrieved his phone and played the recording, of Kia confession. Strick was stunned, "damn, "he said.

"who is that?" He added.

"Kia, her husband is this Africa wh-"

" I know who he is," Strick said slamming his hand down on the kitchen counter. Danjunema and him did business for over 15 years and were close friends. "So, you're fucking his wife?" He asked. June shook his head yes. "Who else know about this?" He asked.

"No one" June said confused.

"You get the spot but under one condition. You must never tell anyone about this." Strick said. June couldn't understand the situation but wanted to live more than being noisy. "say no mo, but I'm gone need that greenlight lifted before I walk outta this building. You know I could lose my life in a New York minute. "Strick smirked and pick his phone up, he sent a group text to all the head of certain hoods to call off the hit. At that moment, the gun was removed from his head."

"Relax, you back at home, won't know harm come yo way!" Strick said, waving the gun man off leaving them alone. "I'll take care of this, it's no longer your business." He said, before waving June off as well. June turned to leave, "wait," strike yelled. "You'll be crown king in a few days. We'll make a show of it this time and put you at the top of the stage. Just remember who really run the show," he said with an even tone. June shook his head, indicating he understood, before turning to leave. When he made it to his car Kutta looked relieved to see him, June got in, and Kutta quickly pulled off. June sat there grinning, "fuck you smiling bout what happened? " Kutta asked.

"Skud we got the crown, bro! They gone make me king." He said happily. Kutta removed one hand from the steering wheel and they shook up. June excitement cause him to be more aggressive than necessary with the clinching of fence." Damn skud, let my mu'fucking hand go." Kutta said, from the pain that shot through his hand. June released it, "my bad skud, " he said. Kutta rubbed his hand and gave June a mean mug," so what they gone do with the bitch?" He asked. June shook his shoulders, "shit I don't know, skud, but I don't think they gone do shit." He said, pondering the same thing. "So, they gone just let her get away with it?"Kutta questioned.

"I ain't gone stand on it but I think so!"

"Damn that's crazy." Kutta added making a turn on 63rd in king drive. "Damn it feels good to be home," June said looking out the window.

"Ya I see they took that greenlight off you!" Kutta said as he glanced at a text from one of the homies.

"Ya we back!" June said, as he thought about how he'd guide them into the future. He thought about cash, leadership style and he wanted to take a few things Cash did right in incorporate them in his kingdom. But a lot was gone change. He would always remember the block boys the hitter and the struggle. Something he felt Cash forgot. June's phone rang; it was Devon, "what good skud?" Devon asked, sounding less aggressive. June smiled inside know the reason for his change of tone." Shit pussy!" June said, still upset with how Devon talked to him earlier. "Look skud, I fucked up earlier. I jumped to conclusion and got disrespectful before have all the information." Devon said, try'na make amends. June laughed inside but, wasn't one to get caught in a power trip, so he let it go." Say no mo... But what's the move." June asked.

"They swearing you in tomorrow night. I'm gone text the address." Devon said.

"Text the address," June said hanging up the line.

"Who that was?" Kutta asked.

"Devon bitch ass, try'na get on a nigga good side." June said. Kutta started laughing, as he parked the car in front of June mom's old house. June kept the house he grew up in; he was too attached to sell it. The block was packed and when they stepped out the sun was beaming, and a few of the lil D's came running over to him. June went in his pocket and pulled out a stack of hundreds and past them out. He wanted to be a commander of the people. Today's little boy is tomorrow shooter. He wanted to hold a spot in their heart, that way when the time came, they'd kill for him without thinking twice. They thanked him and threw up the tre's before running off to play. June and Kutta strolled in the house and sat down in the kitchen. June cast around his childhood home, and memories of his young brother Killa came to mind. It was these memories that made him keep the house. "Remember we would all come over here to eat in the summertime, cause we ain't have food at home." Kutta asked.

"Hell ya, my mom use to talk shit but feed y'all anyways." June laughed.

"On Dave she use to go crazy...." Kutta said hitting the table." The whole time she cooking, then make us say grace after doing all that cursing." He added.

"Them was the days! I miss my nigga's, it only us now." June said. "Who would've ever thought they'd all be gone when we reached the top." He added. Kutta looked over at him," the game can take us at any Moment... Do me a favor, keep me at yo side skud, nobody gone look out for you like I will. " Kutta said from the heart. June glace over at him and shook his head. They'd been through a lot together, and nothing would change that, not money not power. "I know that skud, we been doing this two long for me to switch up now. I know you ain't gone back door me." June said standing up, he put his hand out for Kutta to shack. When Kutta grabbed it June pulled him out the seat and gave him a hug." Love skud "June said.

"Love" Kutta added. At that moment June phone ring with a text. They broke their embrace and June pulled his phone from his pocket. He read the address Devon sent, before putting it back in his pocket. "Skud I'm the man, come tomorrow. You know what we can do with that kinda power?" He asked. Kutta smiled a devilfish smile, "not yet, but we gone find out really soon." He said. June thought about it the world was his, come tomorrow he'd be on top, and began to wonder how much money that could bring. He wanted to hit big and get out. *A year at most and he'd walk away and go legit,* he thought as Black's words played in his head. The game wasn't forever and if he got the chance to walk away ahead, he would.

* * * * *

Black closed the door after the man dropped off their product. She called June to tell him it arrived. "Hello," June said upbeat. Black wounded what had him so happy." That made it." She said.

"Cool, hold it down until tomorrow, I'm gone have somebody come get it. But other than that, I want you to come down to Chicago tomorrow as well, I just ain't try'na put you on the road with that move." He said.

"I ain't try'na be down there, while all this shit gone on!" She said being honest.

"That shit handle. I need you down here so we can discuss the future." He said. Black, trusted June, so it didn't take but a second for her to reverse her decision.

"Oh ok! I'll see you tomorrow." She said, they said goodbye, and she hung up. She wondered how they'd handle things so quickly. When they left it seem like they'd never returned. But now June was happy and asking her to return. Whatever occurred she was glad to hear things were behind them. Even though she didn't want to admit it, she was fond of June and didn't want anything bad to happen to him. She sat down and went on Facebook, as she scrolled down her timeline something caught her eye. Bee Facebook page was up in running. She'd just posted a picture with an older man with the caption "*Africans lifestyle.*" Black checked on the picture and saw it had more than 2,000 likes. A tear fell from her eyes. It was nice to know Bee was alive. She hadn't notice how much she missed her until right now. She liked the picture before commenting, " too cute!"

Almost a second later she got an inbox from Bee. *Sorry, I miss you!* Black was stunned to see this. She quickly responded, *me too I know I let y'all down, and I'll have to live with that the rest of my life.* A second later Bee responded with her number. *(608)-238-0762 call me!* Black stared at the number. Before dialing in pushing call. Her heartbeat sped up as she waited on Bee to answer. "Hello bitch!" Bee yelled into the phone happy to speak to her. "ha girl I missed you so much," Black said. The sound of Bee's voice put her at ease, and things seem normal for the first time since Glory's death. "Black I miss you so much I wanna say sorry for blaming you for what happened. I wasn't in my right mind frame." Bee said something overdue. A tear came down Black's face she'd waited long time to hear these words. She had many sleepless nights hunted by the thought of what could've been different. "Thank you, Bee you don't know how much it, means to hear you say this.... I know I fucked up, and we can't get her back. But we didn't have to turn our back on each other." Black cried.

"I'm sorry Black I truly am, but we'll talk about this when I get back and the states. I have so much to fill you in on.... Okay daddy I'm gone get out the phone right now. " Bee added talking to Danjunema. "I gotta go my father want me to enjoy the sights. Love you bye," Bee said hanging up before Black could ask when she found her father? Black threw the phone on the bed and lay back smiling. A heavy burden lifted of her chest. She spent the last few mouths hurting and missing her friends. And just like that it was all behind her. She couldn't wait to see her friend and catch up on everything they'd missed in each other's lives while upset. Then it hit her she'd have to choose sides between Bee and June. June wanted revenge for the murder's Bee committed. Black knew she'd have to choose Bee side it was only right. She had to get away from June and decided not to go to Chicago. When his people picked up the work, she'd cut all ties and go her separate way. Bee was family, and she wouldn't let a nigga come between them again.

The next day

June woke up and took care of his hygiene before waking Kutta up. "Get the fuck up skud, we gotta go shopping nigga. Tonight, we began our rang as bosses. Kutta shook his head," nah you king!" He said, Getting up. June repeated himself, "we kingpins," he yelled. "We were born bosses nigga!" He added. Kutta laughed," man turn down some nigga it's early as hell, and you screaming and shit." June looked at him grinning, "fuck all that today like Christmas, we going hard until the end of the night." He shouted louder just to mess with Kutta.

Kutta shook his head and went to the bathroom and closed the door. June stood there with a big grin on his face the day had come for him to be the man and it felt wonderful. He was gone get fresh as hell, and make sure he had a hundred thousand on him tonight. He wished he had enough time to get him a chain made. But it was a little too late. But he'd still get it, he had something crazy in mind he was gone fuck the city up. He went in the kitchen and grabbed a bottle water before going to sit on the couch. He lit up the wake in bake blunt, and as he hit it Kutta came out the back. "pass that shit!" He said.

"Damn nigga I just flamed it up." June said.

"Didn't ask that just told you to pass it." Kutta joked putting his hand out for the blunt. June smacked it down and Kutta through up his hands in a fighting stand's. June stepped back and flashed his .9mm " you know I ain't doing no fighting. " he joked. Kutta put his hands up," you got it." He said. June laughed, "nigga you in here playing, when we need to make sure we fucking the city up tonight." June said passing him the blunt. Kutta took it and hit it hard." Then let go!" He said blowing out the smoke. June grabbed his keys and headed out the door.

Once they were in the automobile June pulled off. Heading downtown. They spent the next three hours shopping, before they had everything for the night. As they walked back to the car Kutta headed for the passenger side." Hell, nah it yo turn to drive" June protest. Kutta open the door before "saying we ain't kids, nigga taking turns drive. And I drive most of the time anyway, "he said getting in. " Damn" June mumbled because, he was right. He got in, "we getting a driver tonight then," he said try'na get the last word. " Ion give a fuck," Kutta said just to piss him off. June let it go, Kutta was just fucking with him. They'd done shit like that since kids. He pulled off and headed to the liquor store, where Kutta went to get two 5ths of Hennessey. They were starting the party off early and plan to continue until the nights end. June picked up his phone, called Black but got no answer, he tried again this the same. Next, he called to make sure his cocaine was picked up which it had been. He began to worry about Black and hoped she just didn't have cellular service.

June glanced over at Kutta who'd already opened one of the bottles and was drinking from it. "You grabbed some cups?" He asked. Kutta shook his head yes." Pour me one skud?" June asked. Kutta went in the bag and pulled out the red plastic cup and filled it halfway, before handing it to June." Congratulations skud if anyone deserve this it's you." Kutta said seriously.

"Good looking," June responded. He turned up the music, playing "Grace" *Three hundred fifty thou, times that by two*

New dawn, no roof, I still see the sky

Peace to my grandma, I still see my guys

Turned his back, must've felt let down

Heard a down-set-hut, what you gon' bet now? by Lil Baby. It put him in the mood to eat with his family. To

186

share the wealth with everyone, that's what he planned... When they pulled up on the block it was packed. June parked and they stepped out everyone on the block yelled his name, and some people made their way over to shack his hand," calling him king June." He kinda liked it had a ring to it. Kutta sat on the side of the car and watch making sure nothing looked outta the ordinary. He watched as people flocked to June like the savior of the world and it made him smile. Just knowing one of their own had the throne was what made it so special. He knew June all his life and what he stood for as a man. The future of their block was moving in the right direction and more importantly the future of the BD's was heading in the Right direction. "A skud let's get inside!" Kutta said. And June made his way through the crowd. They walked into the house," Man if every day gone be like this, ion know how good i'ma be at this shit." June said. He liked the attention but wasn't used to it on this scale. He spent most of his life behind the seen taking niggas head off their shoulders. But now he'd have to be a people's person. He didn't know if he was up to it." Nah skud just act like you do around the guys and they'll love you. You got this." Kutta said hitting the bottle. June wanted the kingdom cause he believed he was the best man for the job, and with that in mind he pushed all negative thoughts outta his mind. "I left my cup in the car let me hit that bottle!" He said.

Kutta handed him the drink and went in his bag pulling out his clothing. Before heading to the back to get dress. June set down and slipped on the Hennessey. He began to wonder where would he get his product if something happened to Kia? Would Strick provide it? At that instant, he realized he hadn't asked the proper questions when they met. He planned to fix that tonight. He wanted to know more about how this whole thing worked.

Kutta came out the back-wearing Balenciaga from head to toe. His whole entire was mostly back with white lettering spelling out Balenciaga throughout. He was dripping to hard June thought." I see," June said. Kutta stood tall feeling his self. "This shit light!" He said walking over and grabbed the bottle taking a slip. June went in the back and quickly dress before coming back out. He had on all white Dior, fitting his slim frame nicely. The white air forces ones he loved cause he was a dboy and to him they were timeless. He appeared like the boss he was. Kutta gazed at his brother from another mother and grained. June came out holding 150 thousand in a duffel bag. He had a surprise for Kutta, he planned to get them both a chain made to that demonstrated their states as king. He was getting one of King David and Kutta would have one of King Shorty. He wanted it to be their heads. If they got made the way he envisioned, it would set them apart from others. "I gotta make one more run" he said to Kutta who was sipping on the bottle. He got up without saying a word and grabbed his pistol before heading to the door. June followed him out, and he got in the vehicle pulling off. June went downtown to the jeweler and explained what he wanted done, before leaving the money and headed off.

They rode around smoking and drinking for the next few hours. When night fell June pulled up to the club, and noticed it was packed. They made there was inside, and June was stunned to see the room filled with man. It wasn't a woman in sight, it was at that moment he realized this wasn't a party it was a session. Kutta glared at him with questioning eyes. The room fell silent when they entered June spotted Strick at the back of the room and he waved June over. June walked over with Kutta right behind him. Once they were by Strick, a bodyguard stopped them to inform June to chat with Strick alone. June told Kutta it was alright and walked to the back alone. Strick led him to a small room and closed the door. He turned to face June and smiled, "how are you feeling? " he asked. "I'm cooling," June responded.

"Tonight, is the big night. But I want to get an understanding on a few things before your sworn in. The first thing is I'm giving 30% of everything made from the BD's. I know that sounds like a lot but they must buy product from you, so you'll be making more money than you've ever made in your life." He said. June shook his head to show he approved. "You can get your product from me or you can get it elsewhere. You seem like your already plug with someone with access to the best there is I advise you to use her." He said.

June shook his head, "so y'all just gone let her get away with it?" He asked.

"It's not that simple, there's a lot you don't know, and I advise you to leave this alone as well." Strick said and a firm tone. June let it go, but he wondered what Kia had over Strick. "Ok I got you!" June said.

"You'll pay me my 30% at the end of every month. And you must buy weapons from me alone. Do we have an understanding?"

"Ya," June said. Strick stuck out his hand and June shook it.

"Let's get this session over, then the party will begin." Strick added. They walked back into the packed room and made his way over to Kutta. "You good?" Kutta asked.

"Ya, the party after this!" He answered. The next hour was a blur like an outta body experience. All he could remember was being crowned King, and that's when the girl came in. They walked in all stunning and dressed in underwear. All the females were thick, and some of Chicago's baddest urban model. They'd seem to have been informed who the man of the hour was because they all seemed to want his attention. Ace of spade was flowing, and the DJ was playing nothing but Lil Durk and Lil Baby like crazy. June was smacked from the drinks they had earlier and the bottles he was sipping. Everyone in attendance made their way over to congratulate him and get his number to do business. He now knew what it felt like to be Cash, this shit could become overwhelming if it was like this every day. He decided to worry about that later in enjoy his self-tonight. June went to were Strick and his crew was having drinks and the far corner. The old head sat down while the music played, and a woman performed stripping her top off giving him a clear view of her big boobs. June wanted to get to know the old man a little better, and now was the chance. Strick saw him and waved him over.

"Come have a seat!" He yelled but the music drowned him out. June got the jester and took a seat.

"I got a few things I wanna address." June said leaning in close so Strick could hear him.

"Not now! Let's party." Strick said having had enough of business for one day.

"I get that time is on yo side and you are not in a rush, cause you served this long in the game. But for somebody like me who watched niggas die left and right my whole life, I don't have that time." June said pausing to take a sip of his drink. "I could walk outta here and be killed, so I gotta say this. If something happens to me. My man's Kutta is loyal, and a savage. All I ask is he considered to take my place." June said.

Strick looked at him admiring his confidence, " I could do that! Now go enjoy yourself. Tonight, is about you. Take the time to enjoy the top before you kill yourself off." He said. June looked the old man in the eyes he was right. June had already put himself in a body bag. "Ya I'm gone do that he said getting up and walking away.

June peeked around the club and all the new face made him uncomfortable. It was time to leave, he grabbed the hand of a dancer and asked her did she come with any friends. To which she said "no". He asked her to get a few dancers together who wanted exposure. The feel of a king. She smiled and walked off. June was ready to leave and he planned on taking most of the ladies with him. He walked over to Kutta, who had two ladies in his arms. He was whispering and one of their ears. June tapped him on his shoulder, and Kutta turned to face him " I'mma bout to leave" he said.

"Damn skud the party just getting started." Kutta responded. June turned to the dancer, "y'all coming with us?" He asked more as a statement than a question. They both shook their head.

"Now the party getting started," June added. Kutta smiled, "say know mo," he said. noticed the woman he told to get some ladies standing with ten other models...

They walked over to them, and June asked them "who all drove their cars?" His Range Rover wasn't big enough for all of them. He was lucky they had their own rides. They exited the club, June and Kutta both on point the whole time. They got in the Range Rover with two of the females one up from with June, and the other and the back. June informed the ladies to pull upfront and follow him out. Once they were all line up behind him, he slowly pulled off. When he peeked in the review mirror Kutta head was back, and the girl head in his lap. June began to pull his zipper down and the woman didn't miss a beat when he freed his cock. She held it in her hand before sucking it deep into her mouth causing him to close his eyes. For a second he forgot he was driving. She attacked his tool like she hadn't ate in months. June placed his hand on the back of her head, for the rest of the ride to the hotel. They stopped all action until everyone was inside the suite. Kutta took his two women to the backroom leaving June alone with the rest. The ladies attacked the mini bar. While they ravaged it, June got undressed and sat on the bed stocking his dick until it stood tall. They walked in, a few of their mouths hit the floor. June smiled knowing he was about to have the time of his life.

Chapter Eleven

* * * * *

T he sunshine through the hotel room in Madison. Black looked at her phone and didn't see any more missed called from June. She was thankful he'd given up. She didn't know how long she'd be able to resist his call. Black, missed his company already, and it had only been a few days. He was pleasant to be around, but she chose her sister over him, and felt it was the right decision. She got up and turned on the news and something's stole her breathe; a picture of her face was on the news alone with two cops who were wanted in the killing of Toney Rogers. When they showed a picture, it was Bullet she knew she had to leave the hotel. There was also a picture of June and Kutta, but it was blurry. She pondered how they'd linked the apartment to her but pushed it to the back of her mind for the time being. She hurried and grabbed her things and thanked god she hadn't unloaded the loud from the car like she planned last night.

Black left the room and peeked down the stairs and saw two detectives at the front desk. He quickly made her exit out the backstairs to avoid them. When she exited the building, she saw an unmarked cop car by the front entrance. She quickly climbed and her car and drove off. She drove fast with no destination.

She picked up her phone and called Bee but got no answer. She decided to call June he'd know what yo do.

"Hello," June asked, still in bed with the woman.

"The police looking for me for what happened to Bullet and that shit at my house." She cried into the phone. June heart dropped, "how they know who you was?" He asked. Black kelp crying she didn't know what to do." I don't know but I guess they might've matched my face to the fake ids inside the apartment." She answered.

"So, they looking for us too?" June questioned.

"They got blurry pictures of y'all. I can tell its y'all because I know y'all. But I'm on my way to see you now." She said getting on the expressway.

"Say no more! Call me when you get down here." June said. Black hung up the phone. It was too much going on for her at the moment. But no matter what happened she'd remand solid. The police wouldn't break her and really didn't have much on her. She claimed herself down and relaxed as she went outta town. Thing were going to be okay, and she'd do everything in her power to stay free as long as possible even if it meant cutting her dreadlocks. She stared in the mirror at herself and shook her head, it was years since she wore anything else. But her freedom was worth it. Over the next two hours, she drove deep in thought until she arrived in Chicago. She called June and he told her to meet him on 86th and Morgan. When she pulled up and parked the block was empty.

Kutta spotted her car, and slowly advanced on it from behind. She sat with her back to him. His heart ached for what he was going to do. He pulled his pistol, once he was close, Black reached for her bag on the passenger side and he shot twice through the window hitting her and the back. He opened the door while she slammed over try'na catch her breathe. Black tried claiming across to the passenger side but was shot once more. She turned and looked Kutta in the eyes, surprised to see he was her attacker. "Please, I want say anything!" She pleaded for her life. Kutta look at her and wished he could spare her but couldn't. Blood poured from her mouth as he took her key and shot her once more in the head. Kutta popped the truck, and took the duffel bags, and ran up the street, to a getaway car, and pulled off. His heart was heavy because he'd grown to like Black. But she was a loose end that had to be tied. Now with her outta the way they were in the clear, with no one to tie them to Wisconsin. He pulled up to the trap and one of the lil 'D's took the stolen car to get rid of it. He'd disposal of the murder weapon himself, not trusting a soul to do it for him. June opened the door and couldn't look him in the eyes. He felt bogus for what he did. Black was cool but he didn't trust her with the information she had. Her tear sealed her fate. Kutta walked in the house and closed the door. "It's done!" He said traveling to the back room to take a shower. June shook his head and lay back on the couch closing his eyes and going back to sleep. He was tired from the parting last night.

Two Weeks Later

Bee was back in the states and had called Black nonstop but got no answer. She was beginning to worry. She'd miss a call from her, while with her father. She regretted not answering now. Bee went downstairs and walking in on her mother on the phone. When Kia noticed her, she hung up the line.

"Good morning," Bee said.

"Good morning baby." Kia responded. Bee sat next to her one the couch, "mom my friend not answering her phone, and I'm worried something happened to her." She said. Kia heard the despair in her tone and the expression on her face was innocence. Kia put her arm around Bee and pulled her close to cuddle. "I can have somebody find her for you," Kia said trying to help.

"Thanks mom, I'm so happy and grateful to have y'all in my life." Bee said seriously. "Anything for my baby," Kia said kissing the top of her head. Kia held her, until she decided to go talk to her father," where dad at?" She asked Kia standing. "He left on business this morning." Kia responded. Bee was disappointed he'd leave without her but decided to make the most of the day and have some fun. She planned to head to Madison and her father Rolls Royce with a few of his soldiers. "Okay I'm gone go shopping then," Bee lied. Kia said ok, she had plans of her own for the day. Bee went outside, there were are a group of bodyguards standing in front of the home. She told two of them to come with her, before telling them to get the vehicle. It took them a fee minutes to follow her orders, and they were heading for Madison and know time. She sat in the back strolling through Facebook before searching on Tik Tok for videos to watch.

She plans on showing off, her wealth since she was last seen. When she left she had a few hundred thousand. But now the money in power she possesses was endless. This type of wealth was unknown, and she intended to fit in.

When they reached Madison exited on Seminole. Bee looked out the window, appreciating being home. She'd been across the world, but nothing was as beautiful as the slums of Madison. It was where her heart was. As they drove people stared at the car, and she let the window down so everybody could see who was inside. She smiled and waved at people like she was the President. They drove through Allied Drive and Bee had them make a turn on Rosenberry; she told the driver to stop once they were in the spot she'd been shot. Her adrenaline started pumping as she remembers that night. A smile spread across her face, at how close she'd come to death. But she had someone watching over her and didn't even know it. Sometime god blessed those who were unworthy. He'd took her family away but placed her father in her life at the time she needed him most. She waved for the driver to pull off and he did. Bee picked up her phone and called black again, this time someone answered.

"Hello this is the Chicago police department, whom am I speaking with?" The detective asked. Bee heart drop, for a moment she didn't know what to say.

"Hello?" The officer repeated. Bee took a deep breath before saying "this this Kim Cole, you're speaking with." She said in her most professional voice.

"Kim Cole, what is your connection to this phone line." He asked. Bee didn't wanna answer this question, but she was worried about Black.

"This is my sister phone."

"Oh... I don't know how to tell you this, but this phone was found on a Jane doe in Chicago. I'm not saying this is your sister, but we'd really like it if you'd come to identify the remains." The officer said. Bee heart sink: she couldn't speak. *Not again,* she thought.

"Miss are you there?" He asked.

"Yes, where should I come to." Bee said crying. The police officer gave her the information and Bee hung up. She placed the phone on her lap and screamed. The driver looked back and asked her was she okay. Bee instructed him to take her home. She sat in the back, crying the whole way knowing her sister was gone. She felt it deep inside.

* * * * *

June sat with Kia discussing enterprise. They were inside his vehicle downtown, today Kia was all business. June called and told her, he needed to get his hands on 50 keys, she was interested in how he'd step his order up every time. June sat back looking at her, "I got money for 50 right now, but I need another 20 I'll have yo money and two hours tops." He said. Kia eyed him setting back and his seat, Kia smelled the new confidence coming off him. He just looked different now. "Ok

I got you, just make sure you understand business is business."
She said. June shook his head," trust me I do. Shit I'm try'na get
like you." He said seriously.

Kia smiled, " The kinda money I'm around don't come over
night," she said confidently. Not to put him down, but to tell
him it takes dedication to get where her husband was.

"I know but I gotta start somewhere." He said licking his lips.
Kia loved how sexy he was but wanted to keep things
professional today. "Okay I got you," she said opening the door
and getting out. June rolled the window down, "Kia I need em
like yesterday! " he said, while starring at her fat ass. Kia turned
around, "I'll have them to you within an hour." She said. June
shook his head and pulled off. Over the last two weeks things
had been great. He was getting more orders than he could fill.
It was like he'd been running back to Kia every day for a few, he
contemplated asking her to front him more, but wanted to gain
her trust before asking for too much. He also desired paying for
his product and never have her too much and his pocket. But
right now, he needed a little lead way to make things shake. He
pulled up to Wendy's and picked Kutta up. June dropped him
off to meet Kia." What she say?" Kutta asked getting inside the
car.

"She gone hit us with em." He said, they'd been slipping
everything down the middle. Even though June was the boss he
saw it as a partnership with Kutta.

"When she gone send em?" Kutta asked, and a rush to get
money.

"An hour!" June said as he drove downtown to pick up the chains. He was looking forward to surprising Kutta with the gift. He'd dropped off another 100 thousand for the chains.

"Skud we need to take everything right back to the store after we make this move tonight for that 70 bricks." Kutta said.

"I was thinking the same, but we gotta keep a hundred G's just in case something goes wrong." He said, and Kutta agreed with him. June pulled up to the jewelry store. "What's in here?" Kutta asked.

"I gotta get something for my mom!" June half told the Truth. " coming in with me it's gone be awhile. " June said parking. They made their way inside the store, it was empty. The jeweler came over and gave June a manly hug and shook hands. Kutta watched the exchange with the man and took a seat. June went and inspected the chains; he pulled his from the box's and it caught Kutta eye. He got up and walked over to look at it," bro is that King Dave?" He asked glaring at the chain. June shook his head as the jeweler placed it around his neck. Kutta grabbed the chain which was an iced-out head with Dave face on it. "Bro you gone fuck em up with this!" Kutta said, to busy looking at June's chain when the jeweler pulled out the box with his. June smiled," we gone fuck em up with these, " he said pointing to the jeweler. Kutta turned around in peeped at his and licked his lips. "Damn skud you ain't hav-"

June cut him off," I kinda did." He said.

"This King Shorty?" Kutta said, and June shook his head. The chain was placed on his neck and they looked in the mirror at the falling leader hanging on their neck. June phone ring it was Kia, he thanked god before picking up. "Hello?" He said.

"They at your storage room," Kia said than hung up the line. June smiled knowing he was about to call her an a few hours. The 70 keys was already sold. He just needed to serve them and collect the money. He told Kutta it was time to take care of business, they thanked the jeweler before leaving. When they got in the car, Kutta informed him they need to put a team together cause real bosses wasn't distributing their own product. June thought about it, and he was right, Cash never sold anything. June didn't trust niggas but he had the whole team behind him, and to fuck with him was to fuck with the nation. Yeah, Kutta was right wasn't no need for getting his hands dirty.

* * * * *

Danjunema sat across from Strick who was smoking a blunt. Strick look at him and wondered if he knew his wife was unfaithful. Chances are he didn't which was funny for a man of his status. It was crazy how love could make a fool of the smartest of people. Strick gave up his chase of affection for the chase of dollars.

"So how many will you need this time." Danjunema asked referring to firearms Strick purchased, to supply the city. Danjunema only did business with Strick, giving him exclusive access to the finest weapons. This access allowed them to wage war and keep Strick at the top of the empire. It was the reason he wouldn't betray Danjunema. Their business was more important than one-man life.

"I need 100 AK.47 right now that's it. We ain't at war so ain't too many bodies on the weapon we have at the moment." Strick answer. Danjunema shook his head, without war his arms dill would suffer. But Chicago was a warzone, and in no time, they'd be killing again, and when that time came, he'd make a killing. He made enough money at one war time to last a couple of years.

"You'll have them. Trust me I understand, and if you have any problems you know my number." Danjunema said. Strick got up and shook his hand, before walking out. Danjunema phone rang and it was his wife." Hello," he answered.

"Come home, Bee inside her room crying and won't come out." Kia said nervous. She didn't know what to do, and Bee wouldn't talk to her. Kia called him assuming he'd be able to connect with her. Over the time Bee stayed with them, she had a closer relationship with him than with Kia. Kia was ok with this but while Bee needed help it didn't sit well with her.

"I'm on my way home now!" Danjunema said as he stood to his feet and left with a quickness. He hung up the phone and rushed home to his child. When he made it inside, Bee was locked in her room. Knocked on the door before calling out for her to let him in. Kia stood off to the side, tensed.

Bee unlocked the door for her father, while tear run down her face. She hugged him tightly, shielding a few more tears.

"What the matter," he asked pulling away to look into her eyes. Bee was hyperventilating, so he told her to breathe. She took a few deep breathe before managing to say, "someone killed my best friend," before breaking down again. Danjunema remembered her telling him about how she was reconnecting with a friend while in Africa. She seemed so excited and filled with joy. Bee also said they'd grown up taking care of one another like sisters, and how they'd falling out over the murder of another friend. Danjunema understood there was nothing he could do other than comfort her at the moment. He'd be there for her now and explain, later how loses were a part of the game she'd have to get used to.

A week later

June sat in a room, filled with young soldiers he'd handpicked to run his organization. He picked them fresh out the mud and put them on. He wanted them to grow with him, and hopefully become loyal to him with time. Next to him was his partner Kutta smoking a long fat blunt, while rolling up another on. June casted around the room at all the new faces, things had really changed. He glanced at all the diamond rings on his fingers and it was more proof of his change in States. Life was really good, and he was really enjoying time at the top. With his new team in place, his days were free to fill with relaxation, and sexualization. Most nights a different woman filled the spot next to him in bed. His mother was living in Texas, and no one knew where she stayed but him. Kia was giving him any product he requested at all times of day in night, and they still fucked like animal, whenever she wanted. Life was great, but he missed Kim and Black. Sometimes he thought of all the blood on his hands and got conflicted about this lifestyle. But he wasn't gone give up the crown, at least not now.

"A skud, you good?" Kutta asked. After calling June 3 times without a respond. June looked down at Kutta's hand and saw he was try'na pass him a blunt.

"Ya I'm good!" He said taking the blunt before hitting it. "Let's get outta here." He added, while standing to his feet. He had enough being inside a smoked filled room doing nothing. Without saying a word Kutta stood and followed June out. They stepped outside and the flesh air hit them, June stopped and took a deep breath. When he peeked up, he spotted an armed man quickly approaching, them. Kutta stopped him and reached for his .40 while June did the same.

Bloc! Bloc! Bloc!

June felt the heat as the bullet went through his shoulder, and as a bullet grazed his face.

Kutta returned fire stopped the man from advancing on them.

Boom! Boom! Boom! Boom! Boom!

The shooter ducked behind a van, and Kutta kept firing. June finally got his firearm loose and returned fire. He was hurt, but it didn't stop him from reacting. Kutta looked to his left and stopped a van speeding up the Street with a masked man hanging from the window holding an AK.47 he opened the door to the house before quickly pulling June inside and down on the ground. The second they hit the floor; the house was filled with bullets that seem to go on forever. June kept firing blindly out the door unwilling to give up.

There was a loud screeching sound as the van picked up the shooter before pulling up.

Kutta glazed up and saw the house was a mess. The new members of their team were hiding like cowards.

He glared at June bleeding face and wonder if he'd bed shoot. "You good bro?" He asked standing to his feet and helping June up. June whipped his face, and pain shot through his shoulder.

"Nah I'm hit." He said.

"We gotta get outta here before 12 come " somebody yelled, and everyone rushed outta the house. June throw Kutta the car keys and they jumped inside before pulling off. June began to feel dizzy before passing out.

Kutta looked over at him," you good skud?" He asked. When June didn't respond he sped up and rushed to get him to the nearest hospital.

* * * * *

Big G little cousin got in the back of the van upset he'd missed the chance to kill June. He waited awhile for this chance and was mad he'd fucked it up. After Big G murder he was put in control of their block. He'd been saving money for this moment, and wanted to kill Cash, but somebody beat him to it.

His plan was to wage war on the BD's. But the end would be different this go around with him in command. Big G was a

205

tripper, his goal was always money first. That wasn't the case with him, he got money, as a means to affording war. And now he had it, it was time for revenge. They parked the vin inside garage, before going inside their trap.

"I hit him," Zoo said as he took a seat on the couch. And pushing his locks out his face.

"Ya you hit em G, but ion no if he dead. That bitch as nigga Kutta be on point." Fat head said, taking a seat next to him. The rest of their crew stayed seats.

"Damn, I should've waited until he got closer," Zoo said, standing to his feet. " I rushed it, I wanted him too baby, "he added, pointing his finger like a firearm and pulling the trigger. " man, somebody roll up," he said pulling out an oz from his pocket and throwing it on the table. He was really disappointed in his self. Only if he waited Kutta would've never got the drop on him. Now they knew how he looked, and the element of surprise was no longer his. He got up and went to the bathroom to wish his face, hopefully that would cool him off and help him put this behind him. When he came out the back, they'd flamed up a few blunts. Fat head passed him one knowing it would take the edge off. Zoo grabbed it and took a deep pull before taking it with him to the backroom to face it. He just felt like being alone. He closed the door and sat on the bed still smoking. He thought about when he learned his cousin was murdered. It was devastating, something he'd never forget. Big G took care of the whole family and made sure they were good. When they took him, it changed a lot of people's lives for the worst. Zoo wanted to remind them his life mattered, and the only way to do that was through blood shed, and he planned to shed a lot of it. But

June was the murder he wanted and with time he'd have him. *I got ya cuz,* Zoo thought.

* * * * *

Kutta pulled off from the hospital, after taking June inside. He hoped he'd be okay, but when he left, it didn't look promising. Kutta knew the shorter from high school. He was some kin to Big G. They'd fought a lot at school, and he knew where to find them and decided to pull through their block on 62nd and Michigan. He grabbed his Glock 9 and rolled the windows down.

Boc! Boc! Boc! Boc!

The back window erupted as someone got the drop on him before he could turn on their block. Kutta docked low and pulled off as fast as possible. He didn't know where the shots were coming from. As he speeds up the block his car was repeatedly hit by bullets. He kept his head low and stomped on the gas and peeled off try'na get a way. He sideswiped a few cars praying for the gunshots to stop, which seemed to go on forever. A block and a half away the shoots stopped, and he lifted his head slowly. When he was sure he'd escaped he began to check his body for bullet wounds. Once he was satisfied, he thanked god, for allowing him to make it outta that alive. They were alert and he cursed his self for thinking they'd be lacking. He thought about how Zoo was always on point as a boy, and it wasn't any different now. Kutta was going back to the drawing board, and the next time he came through he'd have a thought-out plan for mask murder. He arrived on the block and looked at his car there was bullet holes everywhere it was a blessed to still be alive. Kutta held his Glock tight as he walked the block to his baby mom's house and knocked on the door.

"Who is it?" She yelled. Kutta began to regret his decision to come over.

"I said who the fuck is it." She replied.

"Gutta!" He said. The door flow open. Andra stood there with her hands on her hips. "what the fuck you want?" She asked rolling her eyes. Kutta walked in the house stepping around her. He went and the front room and took a seat, before hearing the door slam. Andra walked and the room and looked at him like he was crazy. He wasn't playing her no mind; she was upset he hadn't come around the last few months. He hadn't been around but made sure to send over 20 thousand a month.

"So, you just gone show up at my shit? How you know I ain't got company?" She said.

"Where my son at?" Kutta asked without answering her question. Andra knew better than to have a nigga in her crib. It didn't matter how long he was away that was off limits. She stared in his eyes for a moment and noticed he was serious, "he upstairs asleep." She said taking a seat across from him pouting. Kutta glared at her crazy ass and smiled. She was still the most beautiful woman he'd ever known. He loved her but they just didn't get alone. She was a strong-minded woman and wanted to control his life, something he wasn't having. He stood up and went upstairs, and peaked in on his little one, who was sound asleep, before going back downstairs. Andra looked at him rolling her eyes once again. Kutta walked over and bent down placing a soft kiss on her lips. She turned her head away. Kutta grabbed her chain, back towards him and kissed her again. Before pulling away telling her he missed her. Andra kissed him his time letting it be known she missed him as well. Even though she acted tough, she was in love with him. It didn't matter how long he'd been gone without calling she'd be waiting with her legs closed until he came to open them.

She stood up and kissed him while removing his shirt, she hadn't realized how much she'd need him until his moment. Her pussy seemed to be on fire as they smooched.

"I missed you Kutta," she moaned. Andra loved him so much it ached. She pushed the pain and lonely nights to the back of her mind, to enjoy her moment with him. There was no telling when they'd be together again. She didn't want to waste it arguing and fighting. Kutta picked her up and lay her on the couch, he pulled her dress up to her waste and discovered she wasn't wearing underwear. Andra lifted her head looking down at the love of her life, and he kissed all over her legs, until he arrived at her pussy. She grabbed the back of his noggin and forced him to eat her.

Kutta wanted to take his time and make love to her. He shared her fondness even if it didn't seem like it. They just had a complicated relationship. But the love was there. As he ate her, she screamed his name. He continued to lick her clit until she cum. Once she'd stopped, Kutta stood to his feet and Andra began to unzip his pants.

"Mommy" Jr. said coming down the stairs. Andra pushed Kutta away as she heard her son. Kutta sat down, Jr. put an end to the goodtime.

Jr. was 3 years old and when he saw his dad, he got so excited he run to him. Kutta picked his lil man up and hugged him tightly.

"What good lil nigga." He asked.

"Them tre's" Jr. said like his dad taught him. Andra shook her head at Kutta, before, saying, "what I tell you about saying that Jr?"

"Sorry mommy," he relied innocently. Kutta put him down and went in his pocket and pulled out a hundred-dollar bill and handed it to him. Jr took it and gave it to his mommy.

"Kutta you can't buy his love," she said.

"Come on with that bullshit. I ain't try'na buy his love, I'm just make sure he got a few dollars in his pockets." Kutta said. Andra let it go, "how long you gone be here?" She asked.

"I'm gone be around a few days," he said, which made her smile, because he wasn't the type to lie and always kept his word.

"You hungry Jr.?" Andra asked, as he grabbed her phone and took a seat on the floor to play games.

"Ya mommy. I want pizza." He said a little louder than necessary, excited to play the game. Andra went in the kitchen and took out a pizza and put it in the oven. Kutta came in and hugged her from behind. She smelled good and he sniffed her scent. She pushed back against him still horny. She couldn't wait until Jr. went to bed so she could get some dick.

"Kutta why you don't love me?" She asked.

"I do." He replied.

"Why it don't seem like it?" She said turning around to face him. Kutta looked at her, she deserved better, but he didn't know how to provide the love she required. He had a hard time expressing his emotions his whole life, always thought it made him look weak. The love he had for her was no different.

"Andra I'm sorry you feel that way, but I love you more than words can express. He said kissing her on the lips. Andra wish he was more emotional, but she known him long enough to believe he wasn't gone change. She chose to love him as he was a long time ago, and sometimes she forgot this. She stepped away, "I hope one day words can express it before it's too late." She said leaving him standing there alone.

Chapter Twelve

* * * * *

J une opened his eyes and looked around the hospital room, wondering what he was doing there. He tried to touch his face and realized he was handcuffed to the bed. He lifted his head and saw a police officer's standing outside his room.

"A what the fuck y'all got me and handcuffs for?" He yelled at the officer. The detective came and the room smiling, "you under arrest, that's why" he said.

"What the fuck I'm under arrest for?" June asked, mean mugging the cop.

"The shooting dumb ass. What you thought we wasn't gone test for gunshot residue?" The officer said walking towards the bed. "We'd waited a long time to get you June, or king June." The officer added.

June was confused, he didn't know what all they had on him. He wasn't gone do know more talking without a lawyer.

"Ok then take to me to jail so I can call my lawyer!" June said waving the officer off.

"Who the fuck you thinking you talking to?" The officer said, putting his finger in June face. June wasn't dumb enough to talk shit while tied down, so he let it go.

"That's what I thought," the officer said leaving the room. June began to think hard, he wondered why Kutta took him to a local hospital. He must've had no choice if he did, he would've made the right decision. June thought about passing out as soon as they got in the car, and thanked Kutta for taking him to the hospital, even if it meant he spent some time in jail. He'd rather be in jail than dead. June would make bail as soon as he was giving one. He didn't have to worry about that, he'd call his mom and she'd come get him ASAP. He closed his eyes as the meds took over and fail into a deep sleep.

That night

Kutta was laid in bed with Andra she was sleeping, while he lay there in deep thought. He hoped June wasn't upset. He did what he had to to save his life.

Ya he gone understand Kutta thought. He'd called June mother, and told her he was shot and in the hospital. An hour ago, she called him saying June was no longer at the hospital but in the jail. She was flying to Chicago to bail him out.

Kutta rolled over and kiss Andra on the shoulder, and she woke up. "You okay?" She asked.

"Ya, just hoping June get bail, that's all." He said.

"He will this is his first time locked up... And he gone forgive you. You saved his life." She said putting him at ease. Kutta wasn't scared of June, he just felt he'd made the wrong decision by taking him to a local hospital. They had protocol for shit like this, and he went against it, and it didn't set well with him.

"You did the right thing." Andra said kissing him on the lips. She pulled him close and rubbed his back while holding him. He hugged her and closed his eyes.

When he opened them, it was morning, and his phone was ringing. Andra released him and he got out the bed and got it. A smiled spread across his face at the sight of June number.

"What's good skud?" He said.

"Shit skud with my OG, try'na get her to drop me off,but she ain't going." June said.

"Man, skud you know she ain't gone let you outta her sight for a day or two." Kutta joked.

"Where you at?" June asked, wanting to link so they could kick it.

"At my BM crib. Where y'all going I'm gone meet you over there." Kutta said.

"We gone to see my Granny, mom's talking bout she wanna see me before I get myself killed." June said. His family feared for his life, word spread quickly about him being the crowned king. His granny was old enough to tell him about how all the other King life ended young or doing time.

"Say no more. I'm gone meet you over there." Kutta said. He heard, Andra smack her lips and remembered his promises. "A, I'm gone bring Andra and Jr." He added to keep the peace.

"Say know mo, hit me once you outside." June said, and they ended the call. When Kutta put the phone down, Andra was smiling.

"That's why I love you," she said standing to kiss him.

"Why is that?" He asked grabbing her waste.

"You might not always be the most loving man, but you are a man of your word." She said.

"It's the only thing I know. If I say something, I mean it. So, go wake Jr up and get him ready to go." Kutta said, when she turned around, he smacked her ass hard. She kept walking like it was nothing and he licked his lips. Last night they got it in, he loved how freaky she got. It was like the longer he made her wait for the dick, the crazier she went when she got it.

Twenty minutes later they were all dressed and ready to go. Kutta stepped outside making sure the coast was clear for his family to exit. He didn't know if anyone had followed him and wasn't gone lose his family being too comfortable. Once he was sure, he called Andra and told her to come outside. They all got inside Andra BMW, before she pulled off. She'd been to June Granny house many times over, the year and couldn't wait to see the crazy old woman.

Kutta watched the rearview mirror the whole time clenching his pistol. He hated being in the streets with his family, because all the dirt he'd done. The idea of anything happening to them because of him was his worst nightmare. Andra looked over at him and saw how tight he was gripping his pistol and new he'd do anything to protect them. At times she questioned his love but moments like these reminded her of how much he cared. 15 minutes later they pulled up to 71st Green at June granny house, and he was sitting outside with a few of male member of his family standing guard. June was from a family that was deeply tied to the Black Disciple Nation, and Kutta could tell they was proud to have one of their own family running things. He stepped out and Andra grabbed his son out the back seat. June stood up, his arm and a sling and walked down the stairs, "man why you take me to the hospital? " he asked pertaining to be upset. But Kutta knew him too long to fall for the prank.

"Yo ass was about to die my nigga, I just wasn't gone let you die on my watch." Kutta said with raised eyebrows.

"You saved my life two times and one day." June said seriously. Kutta shook his head," I know boi yo ass been lacking, " he joked. Andra walked up holding Jr, " I see you okay big head," she said walking pass him into the house.

June mommy walked out the house. "Kutta get yo ass up here and give me a hug, "she said. Kutta stepped around June making his way up the stairs and hugged her tight." Thank you, baby," he said kissing him on the check.

"You ain't gotta thank me ma" he said.

"Boi you owe me a hundred thousand," June joked. His mother gave him a looked which said ain't shit funny. June put his head down, hoping it would stop what he knew was to come.

"When y'all gone learn, these Street don't give a fuck about y'all? She said. Everyone on the front porch knew better not to interrupt her when she got into one of her molds. They'd all heard it a hundred times, but it wouldn't stop her from reminding them. So, they let her continue." Y'all out here killing like life don't matter to y'all, like its nothing. But god don't forget the sins y'all committing and one day y'all gone pay for them." She added before walking back in the house.

"That was a lot shorter than I expected." Kutta said and everyone laughed.

"I know right "June said taking Kutta a side.

"I know who shot you skud," kutta said once they were alone.

"Who?"

"Man, you remember Corvon from school? He used to have a short cut, but now he got some long dreadlocks." Kutta asked. June shook his head," ya, he go by Zoo now?" June asked.

"Ya that him! He was the shooter. That's Big G lil cuz."

June stood there, thinking, " he gotta go ASAP. " June said.

"I know right. But that might not be easy. Right after I dropped you off at the hospital, I tried going through on a drill and they fan me down the moment I spent the corner. I had to get the fuck outta there." Kutta said.

"What?" June said unable to believe what he'd missed.

"On Dave." Kutta said.

"Say know mo, we gone get that taking care of." June said. "But for right now let's go in here in get something to eat" he added. They entered the house and the smell of food hit Kutta nostrils, pulling him to the kitchen, where he found Jr at the table with a plate, and Andra talking to granny B.

"hi granny," he said walking over to hug her.

"Hi baby where Bullet at?" She asked, use to seeing them tied at the hip. Kutta shook his head as vision on Bullet body on the ground flashed through his mind. Granny B been around long enough to know the look, "not my baby, Bullet?" She said knowing he was gone. Kutta shook his head. Andra looked at him shocked, this was fresh to her. She walked over and give him a hugged. "Why you ain't tell me he got killed?" She asked holding on to him.

"I was try'na forget." He said. Andra witnessed how close they were and knew he was hurting inside. June walked in the kitchen and granny B walked over and smacked him and the face. "Why am I just know hearing Bullet was killed?" She asked upset.

"I ain't even been here that long!" June said rubbing his face.

"That should've been the first thing you said nigga" she said pissed at how deep they were in the streets.

"I'm sorry," June said knowing no excuse would get him off the hook. She shook her head before going to tell his mom. Kutta was hugging Andra who looked at June. "You okay," she asking. June said ya, before going to face the music. His mom would want his head for this lost.

Andra pulled back and looking in Kutta eyes they pain was written over his face." I watched him die" he said as it all hit him at once. "I couldn't react fast enough," he added. Andra didn't know what to say so she just listened. "I watched my best friend get killed," Kutta said still unable to believe Bullet died without him firing a single shot.

"I know if you could have done something you would have. So, don't let this bring you down. You're a strong man and I believe, well I know you'll get through this." She said. Kutta took in her words as she kissed him once more before releasing him. He looked at her once more before going to look for June. Andra watched as he walked away, before going to make him a plate. Jr was buzzy playing and his food, and she took the opportunity to take Kutta his plate. When she walked in the front room, Kutta jumped up, using her as an escape from the lectures Granny B was giving them.

"Man, Granny B on one!" Kutta said taking the plate. He looked back at June and smiled. June was pleading for Kutta to give him an out, but Kutta turned and took his plate to the kitchen. He sat next to his son, who'd made a mess of his self. "Damn Jr the food for yo mouth not ya clothes." He said. Andra walked over to him and picked him up, "boy I can't leave you alone for a second. " she said taking him to the sink to wash his hands. Kutta picked up a piece of chicken and took a big bite.

"A Andra call June in here real quick," he said with his mouth full.

"He try'na get away from Granny B ain't he?" She asked, walking towards the doorway.

"Hell ya!" Kutta said.

"June yo plate ready," She yelled. June jumped up with a quickness and rushed to the kitchen.

"Thank you Andra," he said letting out a deep breath.

"No problem, I know how she can get but she ain't saying nothing but the truth." Andra said. June took a seat next to Kutta, "we gotta get the fuck outta here. I'm gone sneak out the back and walk over a block. I need y'all to come get me cause my mom ain't gone let me leave." June said reminding them of when they were kids.

"Say know mo!" Kutta said still eating his food. June got up and walked out the backdoor. Kutta grabbed his plate as Andra shock her head at him. She didn't like sneaking around but knew better than to go against her man. So, she went alone with the plan. They made their way outside using Jr messiness as an excuse to leave early and was mat with no resistance. Once they were all inside the car Andra waved goodbye before pulling off. She saw June and pulled over picking him up. He jumped and the back with Jr.

"Ooh" Jr said once he saw him. "Yo mommy said you had to stay." He added like June was in trouble.

"Boy stay outta grown folk's business." Andra said. Jr turned and looked out the window at passing cars. "Where we going?" Andra asked.

"ion know, I just had to get the fuck outta there," June said, hitting Jr with a fake punch to the jaw.

"Go to the house we can sit over there awhile," Kutta said watching the review mirror. Andra drove them to the house and they all got out before going inside.

She took Jr upstairs to wash him up leaving them alone downstairs. "So how we gone get that nigga Zoo?" Kutta asked. June shook his head; he didn't know much about Zoo. "First we gotta learn more about the nigga than find the best way to hit em." June said.

"Ya we gotta do something cause just pulling up on that block ain't happening." Kutta said. June smiled at him before laughing, " you thought you was just gone go score?" June said. Kutta couldn't help but laugh, as he remembered how caught off guard, he was when them shots rang out." Hell, ya I'm like this bitch as nigga think its sweet, I'm finnna go through an put somebody down.... Shit I ain't even get a shot off them nigga was all over my ass." Kutta said. June started laughing again. Andra came walking down the stairs," y'all just got me curse out by granny B," she said. June phone ring, he saw it was his mom calling and didn't pick up already, aware what she wanted. Once his phone stopped Kutta phone started. His eyes got wide," this yo OG," he said scared.

"Don't answer that!" June shot back.. It was funny how his mommy turns them from coldblooded killers to scared lil boys. Somethings never changed.

* * * * *

Zoo sat on the passage side of a minivan holding on to a chopper. Behind him was 3 more mini vans filled with gun tooting killers. They pulled up to a basketball court filled with the lil D's and stepped out. Zoo rushed over catching them off guard his machine gun aimed." Don't move," he yelled, and most of them froze, but one turned to run.

Bloc! Bloc! Bloc!

Zoo shot him 3 time and the back his body fell fast and hard. "You not faster than know bullets, boy why is you running?" Zoo sang Tee Grizzley song, while laughing. "Anybody else wanna run? I'm giving heard starts." He asked as his crew made their way onto the basketball court. He waited a few seconds and when no one responded, he made them all get down on the floor. Once they were all face down, he had them executed. Zoo went in his pocket and took out a rag with RIP Big G on it and placed it over one boy blood and brain standard head, before they slowly made their exit.

They pulled off once they were all inside, Zoo was sending a message, that if you took one of his he'd take a few or yours. He wanted June to feel his pain and regret his lost. Until then he'd keep sliding through their hood killing anyone in sight. Age or sex didn't matter to him, anyone could get it. Zoo was a clod hearted killer, and once he was on a mission there was no stopping him. June was his tragic now and he'd kill him, even if it took years.

June's name rang bells, but that didn't matter to Zoo, he wasn't going off names he was gone off body count and he had more than a few. He didn't give a fuck who June was he'd violated, and it would cost him. "Let switch cars and slide through another one of their spots." Zoo said still ready to put in work.

* * * * *

June sat downstairs with Jr watching TV while Kutta was upstairs doing god knows what when his phone ring.

He picked it up when he saw it was Strick, "hello," he said turning the channel. "We got a big problem; I need to see you at the sandwich shop ASAP." Strick said in a calm but firm voice.

"I'll be there soon" June said and Strick hung up the line. June Wonder what the problem was, as he got up to go get Kutta. When he walked up the stair's Jr followed behind him, he was really happy to be around his stepfather. And followed him everywhere he'd went, June heard Kutta and Andra talking through the close door before knocking on it.

"Come in," Andra yelled. When June entered the room they was laid up snuggling.

"I see y'all." He joked.

"Whatever!" Andra said giving kutta a kiss on the lips. June smiled it made him happy to see the joy she had when Kutta was at home.

"What's the move?" Kutta asked wanting June to get the fuck out so he could get his freak on. He looked at Jr who was now holding June hand and smiling for no apparent reason at all and thank god for giving him a family. He need to spend more time with them, and veiled to do just that." The old head want a meeting ASAP, and I need you to watch my back." June said.

Andra shook her head believing this would take Kutta away. She hated the fact that he was in the streets cause at any moment they could come calling and he'd always answer.

"Say know mo, give me a minute and i'mma meet you downstairs." Kutta said. June and Jr left the room and went downstairs. Andra pushed his arm from around her and, got outta bed. She was mad and had every right to be. But he had business to take care of. "You always do this shit." She said." You come over her and spend a few hours, a day or two at most, and walk out on us for the streets. " she continued. "I hate that you put this shit before your family, and what's fucked up about it is you don't even see how much it hurts us to not have you around " Andra said looking at him with hate in her eyes. Kutta didn't know what to say, so he stood up and began to get dress while she starred a whole through him. He felt her eyes locked on him, as he put his shoes on. "So, you ain't gone say nothing?" She asked.

"What you want me to say." Kutta asked, standing up and facing her. She shook her head and whipped away a single tear that fell from her eyes. "Say you gone stay with yo family shit, say you gone choose me and your son for once," she said cocking her head to the side. Kutta looked at the beautiful woman and wished he could give her what she desired, but he'd made a commitment to protect his friend and he had no plans of reneging on that. He walked up and kiss her lips, before walking out the room without saying a word. On his way down the stairs, he heard her cries as she broke down.

June heard her as well, when he saw the stress on Kutta's face it was clear what had just taken place. Jr heard his mommy crying and ran to see what was wrong with her.

"You ready?" Kutta asked in a low tone.

"Ya," June said and they headed for the door. Kutta opened it and they stepped out slowly walking to the car and Kutta took the drivers sit of Andra car and they pulled off. June didn't say a word, allowing Kutta to collect his thoughts. They'd been arguing over him leaving and he felt bad to cause Andra pain. June understood how much she loved him; she only wanted his love in return. Kutta made the drive to the sandwich shop deep and thought. He wanted to be there for his family and planed on showing Andra, he loved her and wanted to spend a lifetime with her.

"A skud, I need you to help me find a house for Andra. I want something nice and in Illinois somewhere docked off." Kutta said. He wanted to show Andra he was all in and one way to do so was to finally move them out the ghetto.

"I got you, I'm gone call my people and have them put a few places together for you to look at." June said.

They pulled up to the sandwich shop and got out. When they walked in the placed was filled with young man seated around. There was over 50 of them. June wonder what was going on as they made their way to the back. They found Strick sitting in a small office smoking. "Have a seat" he said, and they both took the chair place in front of the desk. Strick sat back and pulled on his blunt before saying anything.

"We got a problem," he finally said." Someone been coming through our blocks shooting and killing anyone in sight " he added. "This is a problem because 5 kids were just killed for playing basketball..." He paused to let his words sink in." The police are calling this a gang war, and they want to put an end to it before more blood is shed. This is an issue because they start looking into us and might come down with an indictment. If this happens there's a chance, we can all end up and prison." He said. Kutta looked over at June to see his expression and it was emotionless.

"So what do you want us to do about it?" June asked.

"I have 50 of our best shooters upfront... They have been told to follow all your orders and to watch over you until this thing is over. I want you to press hard over the next few weeks and end this thing." He said. June stood up to leave with Kutta following behind him." Wait I have something to show you," Strick said stopping them and their tracks. He stood up and told them to follow him to the kitchen. When they strolled in there was gun everywhere. Kutta eyes light up at the sight. "Here, choose anything you want. But know it's gone to cost you." Strick said.

June looked around, he picked up a few weapons before he grabbed a Mac 11." Kutta get whatever you want." June said and watched as Kutta went around looking. "Can you get me more of these?" June asked holding up the Mac 11's

"As many as you'd like." Strick said.

"Get me 51 of em than" He said, his mind on the war games he was getting ready to play. He loved war, it put him at ease. "That's gone cost a nice penny," Strick said with a straight face, but smiling on the inside.

"Good thing I'm making more than a few Penny's" June said. "Just put whatever it is on my tab and I'll have it sent here before the end of tonight." June added.

Strick had no problems with this at all. He was in this game to make money and war was where he made the most of it. Kutta picked up and FN and fell in love. He thought about busting Zoo brains with it and smiled it was time to play.

Strick sat and his office 15 minutes after they left. He picked up his phone and called Zoo. The phone ring a few times before Zoo answered.

"What good?" Zoo asked.

"How you feeling, nephews" Strick asked. Zoo wasn't his real nephew, but he thought of him as so. He'd known his father from back and the days. Zoo father use to be Dell Viking and when they flipped, he went to the other side. This is where their friendship should have ended but it didn't. Strick saw the benefit of having connections on either side, and they keep in contact over the years. Their relationship allowed Strick to supply both side with firearms. He used to do business with Big G but once he was killed, he started to supply Zoo. He was able to play both side because everyone believed he was outta the game. But he was behind the scenes pushing for conflict he could benefit from selling illegal weapons.

"I'm coolin try'na see when you gone let me come through. Shit I got a 100 to blow." He said talking about 100 thousand. This made Strick smile.

"That's what I'm calling about it's ready you just gotta come pick it up" he said leaning back in his chair.

"Cool cool I'm gone slide through in about an hour." Zoo said.

"Ok just come to the back." Strick said wanting to avoid being seen with him. Strick got off the phone with Zoo before calling Danjunema.

"Hello," Danjunema said.

"I need you to arrange me a trip to Africa for the next few months." Strick said. Wanting to be long gone while the war took place, in case the feds come down, he wouldn't be easy to locate.

"When are you try'na leave?" Danjunema asked more than willing to help out his old friend.

"Tonight!" Stick replied.

"I can arrange that. Will you be needing protection for the stay?" Danjunema asked because Americans were targets for kidnappings and ransoms.

"Ya, I need some." Strick said.

"Ok then how about you stay at my place until you're ready to return. That way you'll be safe, and people will know you a friend of mine."

"Thank you I'll like that."

"No problems my friend. I'll have the place ready for you and the jet will leave at 10pm, is that fine?"

Strick thought about if it was more than enough time to have everything in order.

"That will be great. thank you and I owe you one." Strick said.

"No problems and you know I'll cash in on that favor." Danjunema said, understanding how valuable a favor from Strick was.

"I know, thanks once again." Strick said and they ended the call. Strick planned on spending the next three weeks in Africa enjoying life while they killed over nonsense. If was good to be woke and pulling strings like a puppet master.

The next day

It was 8am and June was on his way to get Kutta from Andra house. He'd dropped him off last night after getting to know some of the shooter Strick had supplied. Last night while at a hotel he'd called his people and had them arrange for Andra to see a few homes and the suburbs.

He pulled up outside and beeped three times. A minute later Kutta came out and got in the car.

"What's to it?" He asked as he closed the door.

"Shit skud gotta go get up with dude em to get a plan together. We gone slide through a few different hoods all at once." June said, wanting to start things quickly as possible. He drove to 55& Blackgate, upped protection since they were last shot at. A few men were on each corner on watch and stopping any car that didn't look former. June called ahead of time and told them he'd be pulling up and his black Range Rover. But he was stopped anyways, "what the fuck they on," Kutta asked. June looked over at him smiling," they on point," June said as they give them the ok to pull through. He parked in front of an old house and got out as the shooter stood outside. They stole 10 vans and put them a block over like June instructed. He looked at them and all black and smoking blunts ready for war. *I loved this shit,* June thought ready to demonstrate to Zoo how to get down.

June walked up and addressed the crowd, "this how we gone do it 5 men to each van, one person drive and the others hop out and shoot anything moving. Anybody over 14 get it no questions asked." June said. When he was sure his instruction didn't bother them the slightest bit he continued.

"Anybody over 14 boy and girl?" One of the shooters asked for verification. June though about it a moment, before changing his mind. "No women," he said.

June told them all the hoods they were to hit before they loaded into vans and head off on the mission while Kutta and June stayed behind. Kutta followed June inside a little disappointed they wasn't going on the drill. This boss lifestyle was taking away the enjoyment of the game. Kutta treasured getting his hands dirty and his new position was stealing that from him.

"Man, we should be out there sliding," Kutta said closing the door behind them.

"Ya I'm with you on that, but we gotta think like bosses and that means missing out on some shit." June said. He believed this was the right decision, but it just felt wrong. He craved being on the front line with his men and this went against everything he believed. He sat back on the couch and relaxed, knowing this block was safe with all the secret watching over it. He was in the hood, but he couldn't of been more safer anywhere else. "Damn skud this shit lame," Kutta said taking a seat next to him.

"I know," June replied with closed eyes.

Chapter Thirteen

* * * * *

A black van crept up the almost empty block. Two man stood on the corner talking and didn't notice the van as it got close. Only when they heard the slide door open did they spot the masked man as they jumped outta the back.

Both men took off running in different directions and the shooters gave chase. They didn't waste bullets shooting at a moving target instead they chased them until they were close enough to hit their target with ease. The first shoot caught up with his target in an alley when he ran outta breath the man turned and put his hands up. "Come on don't shoot me I got kids," he pled for his life. The shooter behind the mask smiled. "Fuck yo kids gotta do with me?" He said before shooting him 4 times and the stomach. The slugs knocked him to the ground but didn't kill him. The shooter slowly walked over to him while he screamed and put his foot over his chest before shooting him and the head once. The other two shooters was still, and a foot chased with the other man who had a lot more stemma. He run low to the ground and keep turning conners and jumping fences. One of the shooters began to get tied, so he stopped and aimed, as the man run up the middle of the streets.

Boom! Boom! Boom!

Two of the rounds struck the man and the back and he fell over before getting back up and running outta one of his shoes. The shooter that discharged his weapon gave up and run back to the van and jumped inside. The other killer wasn't giving up just yet. The guy running for his life began to slow down as he lost blood. His mind wanted to keep moving for him to survive but his body gave out and he fell over smacking his face against the curve which knock him unconscious. The shooter stood over him placing the weapon to the left side of his chest and pulling the trigger twice. Before running off to the van which speed away.

Meanwhile

A group of brothers sat on the porch smoke the first blunt of the day and talking about last night game. They relaxed their minds before the tough day head of them. Today was their family reunion, and it was gone be some type of drama, and fighting amongst them. When a van pulled up and four man jumped out aiming Mac 11," what the fuck- " one of the brothers began to say before he was cut off when a bullet struck him in the neck cutting off his wind supply. He fell to the floor holding his wound but quickly died from his injury's. The man continued to shoot until there was no longer anyone alive on the porch before getting back in the van and speeding off.

A block over

Inside the black minivan the shooter search for any sign of victims, but the block looked empty. "Damn skud, ain't nobody out here," the driver said while he crept up the street. Their minds were in the same state, wondering how the fuck they ended up with the empty mission. Out of all the blocks theirs was dead.

"This some bitch as shit," one of them said taking his mask off and relaxing his grip on his Mac 11. Once they made it to the corner one of them said spend the block again before they give up. Not wanting to come back without a story and a body count the drive did just that.

"Damn he yell," once they turn the corner and still saw nothing. He slowed down preying somebody anybody would come walking out their house.

Boom!

A man stepped out from behind a car and blew the driver head off with a 12 Gage shoot gun. His brain blew on to the shooter sitting in the passenger seat as the car rolled down the block. 4 other men stepped out the cut rushing the van firing into it with Ak.47 from all ends, the shooter inside didn't stand a chance against the ambush attack. Over 100 rounds were shot into the van, and when they stopped everyone inside were hit multiple times. The ambushers took off running while one laugh could be heard, it sounded like a satisfied hyena.

Meanwhile

A man stood in front of the corner store smoking, while holding a pop in his other hand. He watched a teenager make his way up the block holding a basketball when a man approached him from behind and shot him once in the back of the head. The ball and his body hit the floor almost at the same time. The man dropped the pop in shock at what just took place in front of his eyes. He watched the shooter jump inside a black minivan and it speed his way. His mind said run but his feet wouldn't move. At all seem to take place and slow motion, the van stopped before and the last thing he saw was the barrel of a gun before an explosion. The van pulled off slowly, and they made their way a few blocks over. All the shooter jumped out while one ran and got the getaway car, another poor gasoline all over the stolen van and set it on fire. They waited and watched it go up and flames before jumping in the getaway vehicle before they speed off, mission complete.

* * * * *

Zoo phone rang on the nightstand, and he reached over and grabbed it.

"Hello," he said sitting up in bed, and glancing at the beautiful woman next to him.

"What?" He yelled hearing the bad news. The girl woke up looking scared. Zoo got up and walked out the room while being informed of what happen to a few of their hoods. He hung up the phone and went to get dress. *These hoe ass niggas wanna play he though.* While grabbing his pistol and rushing to leave the T.H.O.T house. She watched him without saying a word, because he'd never explain to her, so why ask. Zoo walked out the front door and spotted the black minivan when the engine start. He pulled his pistol and let off two shots.

Bloc! Bloc!

The rounds hit the front windows but didn't hit anyone inside. Zoo claimed the fence and run down the gangway. The van speed up and 4 people jumped out the back. Zoo was familiar with the area and made a left turn and run into an abandoned house. He locked the door behind him and run to the basement.

The 4-man hit the corner and didn't see him. They looked around confused.

"He ain't far "one of them said.

"Go make sure he ain't in that house." Another commanded while running in the alley looking into the garbage cans. Two approached the house guns aimed. One tried the door and found it locked.

"He in there?" The one from the alley asked.

"It locked," they both yelled back.

"Kick it end than." He replied. But they all stopped in their tricks at the sound of sirens.

"Damn, we gotta go," he added running back to the van and they followed closely behind him.

Zoo sat in the basement his firearms aim at the upstairs door. If anybody came close, he was going start firing without thinking. He put the gun down when he heard the sound of 12 (police). *Damn, I'm stuck here for a while,* Zoo thought. He couldn't wait to get to the field to put in some work it was time to get to it...

* * * * *

June was watching TV while Kutta was in the back asleep. He'd been watching the breaking news stories of the shooting. It put a smile on his face to see the shooters wasn't fucking around. It pissed him off when he noticed one of the minivans had been ambushed and everyone inside was dead.

It was something about losing men under his control he'd never get used to. June turned off the TV and went in the kitchen to make something to eat. As he made a TV dinner, he thought about the fact Zoo must've survived the hit cause the only thing reported on 62nd in apply heart was shoots fired. The female who's house he was leaving outta was an old friend of Junes, she'd set up the hit, but under the conditions he wouldn't be killed in her home. It was crazy they had the drop on him and missed the chance. But if he didn't put two and two together about the setup, they'd get another chance. June sat down at the table with a lot on his mind. This war shit was fun and all, but if it went on too long it would fuck with his money, and he wasn't trying to have that happen. June lit up a blunt and hit it hard as hell, deep in thought. He began to think what Cash would do, and that's when it hit him, Cash still got money while beefing. He'd let them defend the land, while he sat back, in the suburbs pushing his work through others. June planned to do just that, and while things got out of control in the city, he'd be in Beloit chilling. June got up grabbed his pistol and went to wake Kutta. When he walked in the back Kutta was laid back on the bed smoking a blunt, he'd been thinking about how much things change since they been at the top. He wanted in on the action, but that wouldn't happen no time soon, so he pushed it to the back of his mind.

"You wasn't watching the news?" June asked. Kutta shook his head no, taking another pull. "what I miss?" He asked.

"Them young boy put in that work... But missed the nigga Zoo." He said, Kutta shook his head disappointedly. "Man, that's why we should've been out there. I know I would've put his ass down." Kutta said. Pleading his case to be out in the field. June new what Kutta wanted and decided to give it to him. "I'm shooting out to Beloit, after I bust a few moves you can run the operations down here with his beefing shit. I can tell it's killing you to watch from the sidelines." June said.

Kutta eyes got wide, with blissfulness. "That's what I'm talking about. I'm gone take care of this shit and a few weeks max," he said getting out the bed grabbing his 9.mm. June shook his head at him, he was a hitter and loved it. June on the other hand was slowing down and getting tired of the bloodshed. After having Black killed it just didn't sit well, with his conscious. And he didn't want to spend the rest of his life in the game. The conversation he had with her was always in the back of his mind.

It was up to him when he left the game, no one else. Kutta wasn't at that point and June wanted to let him prove himself, and hopefully when the time came, he'd advocate for Kutta to be the next king.

"I'm gone get on top of thing right now!" Kutta said heading out the room and on the block." June followed him, and when he exited the house Kutta was barking orders to foot soldiers. June called him over to the car, "be safe bro, if you need anything call me." June said, getting inside in rolling the window down. He looked at Kutta and begin to second guess leaving him behind. "what god skud?" Kutta asked.

"You should come with me!" June said. It was something about leaving that felt different this time.

"I'm good in the field, this where I wanna be." Kutta said. It was apparent June was worried about him. It was understandable because they were the last of their original crew. But Kutta wasn't feeling, hiding and now sliding. He wanted to leave it all on the field win or lose.

June looked at him and noticed his mind was made up. "Stay on point and check in with me before the end of the night. If shit get too hot out here, just hop on the highway and link with me." June said. They shook up and June pulled off slowly.

He called one of his runners and told him to be on standby. June wanted to get his hands on enough bricks to last a few mouths. He'd front them to the guys and collect his money, while outta town until the war was over. He called Kia and place an order for 100bricks, before picking up his phone and looking through his contact for a bitch to kick it with until things were clear in Chicago. When he came across Naomi's number, and thought about how good her pussy had been. June called her number, and she picked up on the 3rd ring.

"What good boi," she said sounding sexy as hell.

"You I'm try'na come get you," June said.

"Now why would I fuck with you after how you played me last time?" She asked. June forgot all about the last time he'd seen her, so much happened in his life since then.

"Man, I'm sorry, I been thinking about you a lot since then. I been wanting to apologize but didn't have the courage to call until now. " June lied.

"It's cool where you try'na take me?" She asked forgiving him.

"Wherever your heart desire." He said, rubbing his dick through his pants.

"You know where to find me call me when you outside. " she said excitedly. June hung up the line and laid it on his lap. All he had to do was keep his cool for a few months in than he'd leave the game behind. *It was time to start planning his exit* he thought.

Two hours later

June pulled up to Naomi's house and called her. She picked up and told him to come inside. He made his way inside and check it to make sure they were alone. Naomi looked at him and shook her head, while he walked around the house like it was his. When he was satisfied, they were alone he relaxed.

"I told you last time I wasn't that type of bitch," she said smacking her lips. June looked at her she was wearing a pair of shorts that hugged her thighs so tight, it showed the outline of her fat pussy.

"I told you it wasn't about you it was me just being alert. " he said licking his lips. Noemi looked at him he had too much drip without even trying. His swag was what made her give him a chance in the first place. "You said you was gone take me where my heart desire, and what my heart desired his this." She said reaching for his dick and rubbing it through his pants. June wanted the same thing, so he picked her up and sat her down on his lap on the couch. She began to kiss him on the neck, and he took off her shirt, she lifted her arms to help him get it off. Once he threw the shirt on the ground, he began to suck and kiss all over her chest. Naomi was in heavy, he just knew how to touch her, and make her go wild. She got off his lap and undressed, June was right behind her, and within seconds they stood before each other naked. June wanted to taste her, so he had her lay back on the couch. He took his time licking her everywhere but her spot. She grabbed his head focusing him to lick it. June attacked her sucking hard on her clit, Naomi jumped at the wonderful feeling. He took this as a sign to keep going, and he did just that. He licked her to orgasm. June wasn't in the mood for head, so he entered her driving halfway inside her. She screamed in pleasure, pushing all the way out and slammed in, causing her to have another orgasm.

Her pussy gripped him so tight his toes curled. He fucked her nice and hard for another twenty minutes before he had to slow down to stop from busting. He began to think about something else to hold off but when she tightened her cat around him, he closed his eyes in released a load deep inside her.

Naomi looked at him in amazement, he was the best she'd ever had hands down. June got up and went in the back to wipe his dick off. Naomi came inside the restroom with him getting in the shower. June didn't say nothing to her before putting his dick back inside his pants. He went back upfront and sat on the couch. He heard the shower running before it went off. June thought about his plans, and now that he'd gotten his nut off, he began to come to his senses. Naomi didn't have a place in his future, he got up laughing at how funny it would be to leave her with nothing but a wet ass. June got off the couch and opened the door leaving the house. When he walked outside, he was still smiling. He never saw Marvell behind the building door,

Bloc!

The shot to the back of the head, blew his brains out and sent his lifeless body slamming face first onto the pavement.

"My sister told me to give you that pussy!" Marvell said running off. June might've thought Naomi was a joke, but she didn't. He'd wrote her off as another stupid bitch, but he should've been aware of the snake.

To be Continued…….

Team Savage III

"Be aware of the Snake."